The Perfect Dinner

The Perfect Dinner

Fine Food Cooked With Foil

Jacqueline Mallorca

Illustrated by Deborah Hum Choy

FAIR OAKS PRESS • SAN FRANCISCO

Acknowledgments

There is more to publishing a cookbook than having a compelling idea and developing a lot of recipes around its theme. It takes support and encouragement to bring it all about. For their help, I gratefully acknowledge the contributions of Mark Adams, Celia Bakke, Kris Balloun, Paul Berg, Debbie Choy, Gail Ellerbrake, Heidi Gintner, Dotty Hardberger, Gary Jones, Sandy Kriegsman, Richard Lucchesi, Elspeth Martin, Domini Williams and Betty Rommel at Regent Publishing Services, Kathy Schermerhorn, Chuck Williams, Andrew Ziobro and, in particular, Don Roberts of Fair Oaks Press.

Published by Fair Oaks Press, Box 192871, San Francisco, CA 94119

Mallorca, Jacqueline
The perfect dinner : fine food cooked with foil / Jacqueline
Mallorca ; illustrated by Deborah Hum Choy.—1st ed.
p. cm.
Includes index.
ISBN 0-9658811-8-0
1. Cookery. 2. Aluminum Foil. I. Title.
TX652.M254 1999 98-73198
641.5'89–dc20

Library of Congress Catalog Card Number: 98-73198
First Edition

Printed in Hong Kong

10 9 8 7 6 5 4 3 2 1

Contents

The Perfect Dinner

Once while I was walking in a leisurely but not dawdling way from Vézelay to Avallon (it was only about sixteen kilometers, but I managed to spend a good five hours covering the gentle empty roads), I discussed, with an intensity seldom given to conversation and very rarely sustained without boredom for so long a time, the subject of The Perfect Dinner.

—M.F.K. FISHER
from An Alphabet for Gourmets

Foreword
Fine Food Cooked with Foil

DINNER is a meal that aspires to perfection. Someone once described it as "supper by candlelight," which underscores its special nature as an *occasion,* and one worthy of the best food possible made with the freshest ingredients available. The perfect dinner can be as uncomplicated as a bowl of thick, creamy soup served with salad greens and oven-fresh bread, or as grand as four courses with a crown roast of lamb as its centerpiece.

A dinner's praises are more often sung for what occurs at the table rather than what went on in the kitchen. In fact, a perfect dinner should be perfect from the cook's point of view as well. To the cook, it begins with ease of preparation within a reasonable amount of time, continues at the table over nourishing food (and nourishing conversation) and concludes with a minimum of cleanup.

I remember my friend Jim Beard, the late "dean of American cooking," speaking of a dinner at the home of some people he hardly knew. It seems he scarcely saw his hosts all evening because they were kept so busy in the kitchen. A bit peeved, he departed at evening's end without getting to know them any better. To him, this was not dinner, but rather a waste of good food.

Whenever I want good food on the table fast, with the least amount of preparation and cleanup (which is most of the time, whether I'm cooking for one or for six), I bless the inventor of aluminum foil. In cooking with foil, I can relax at the table while packets and foil-lined pans prepared in advance follow one another into and out of the oven at regular intervals. And need I add that these handy little packets are disposable? Unless you happen to enjoy scrubbing pots and pans, this is a definite bonus. That is what this book is about: simple recipes for fine food, cooked with ease in—as well as on and under—foil.

Foil-packet cookery makes all sorts of culinary conjuring possible. It is the natural descendant of *cuisine en papillote,* the French technique of quickly steaming foods individually wrapped in specially treated parchment paper. In professional kitchens, the open sides of each packet are still laboriously folded together and then painted with egg white to ensure an airtight seal. But when the packet is made of the inexpensive foil, this simple method becomes accessible to today's cook and is far more easily executed.

Quickly folded and crimped shut, foil conducts heat to its contents without delay, so many entrées cook in only ten minutes. With a fish fillet or chicken breast providing the moisture needed, very little fat is required. Best of all, fresh foods retain their tantalizing aromas and natural flavors—as well as their nutrients. Nothing is lost.

All too often we reserve our best cooking for dinner guests, but you can easily cook an exceptional meal for one or two with foil packets. And when cooking for more, the results are identical, regardless of the number of packets. (We've all discovered the hard way that even tried-and-true recipes have a way of going wrong when multiplied in a pan.)

Another great advantage lies in preparing the packets for several different dishes ahead of time. For a meal with several courses, I've found that cooking one course in foil packets, the next in a foil-lined pan, and so on, works especially well. Here are the essential guidelines to keep in mind:

- *Packets can be assembled and refrigerated up to three hours in advance. Bring them to room temperature before they go into the oven, or add two minutes to the cooking time.*
- *Always cook foil packets in one layer on one baking sheet positioned on the center rack.*
- *Bake only as many packets at one time as you can reasonably handle.*
- *For most dishes, preheating the oven and baking sheet is critical to the recipe's success. (Allow 10 to 15 minutes for an oven to preheat.)*
- *Although some experts claim that the shiny side of foil will deflect a certain amount of oven heat while the dull side absorbs it, I've never detected any difference with packets made either way.*

Every culinary technique has its strengths as well as its limitations. The foods that cook best in foil packets are produce, fish and scallops, chicken and some cuts of meat. Even so, foil can play a helpful role in roasting meats and vegetables, baking breads, cakes and tarts, and even cooking rice. Sealing a baking dish with a piece of foil is hardly a new idea, but the technique is underutilized. I've found that rice and lentils are easily cooked in a foil-covered bowl in a hot oven, and even better, this simple technique can be used to make a really good risotto. And of course, lining a baking or roasting pan with foil will minimize sticking and reduce cleanup.

The recipes in this collection are but the tangible components of what could be the perfect dinner. While the dinner table has always been the center of fellowship and celebration, there is an aspect to dining that we sometimes lose sight of: the very personal pleasure of it. Mary Frances Kennedy Fisher, that most delightful of writers on matters of life in general and the table in particular, wrote that "sharing food with another human being is an intimate act that should not be indulged in lightly." She understood perfectly that cooking is an expression of love and care, with benefits that go far beyond simple sustenance.

Jackie Mallorca

Techniques
for Cooking with Foil

TIGHTLY SEALED in a hot oven, foil packets function as individual little pressure cookers: Inside each one, the ingredients' juices create aromatic steam, swelling the packet like a balloon while the food quickly cooks. A little olive oil or butter will keep the contents from sticking to the foil and also adds flavor.

The Foil Packet

The D-shaped foil packets I make are similar to the parchment packets of classic *en papillote* cooking and simple to prepare: Tear off a length of foil (12" width), and lay it flat on a work surface. Then spray its center area with a little oil, or smear it with butter. Place the ingredients to one side of the center of the foil (1).

Fold the foil over the ingredients. Then, starting at the crease, fold and crimp the open edges tightly together to create one long curving edge, leaving plenty of air inside (2 and 3). Transfer the packet to the preheated baking sheet.

Once the food has cooked, place the packet on a dinner plate, and slit or snip open the long, folded side. Withdraw the foil, leaving the food on the plate (4).

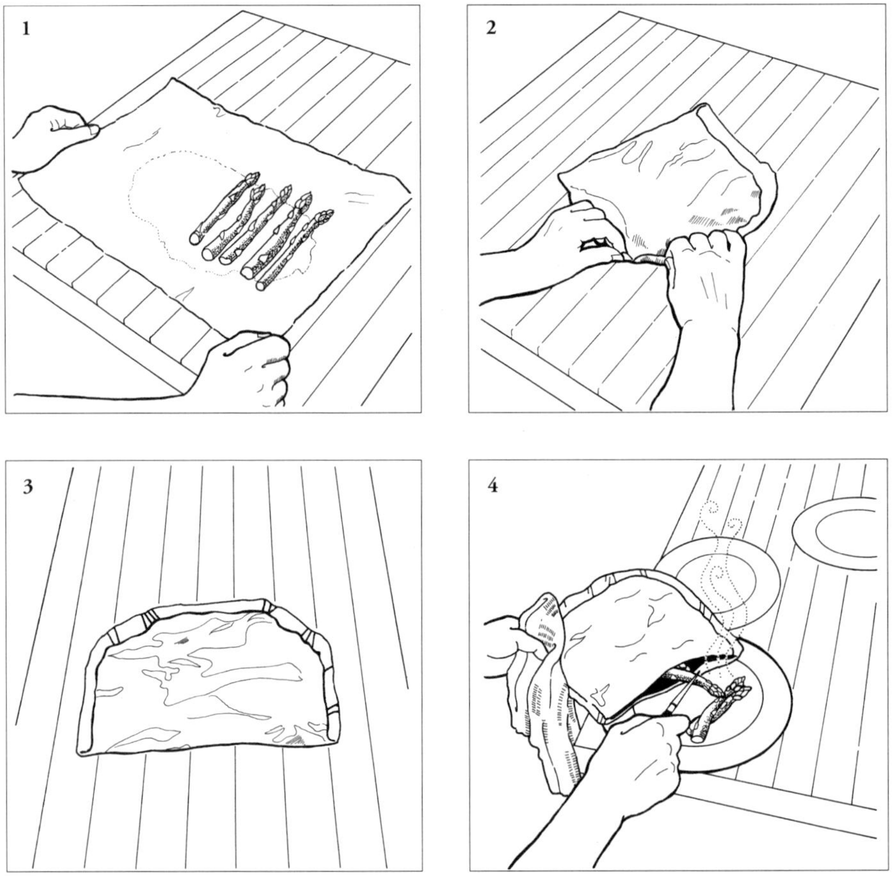

An Ice Cube

Some vegetables are less endowed with the natural juices that create steam for successful foil-packet cooking, and meat stews always require additional liquid. This is a problem with a clever solution: Rather than attempting to pour even a small amount of water into the packet, place a cube or two of ice in it. The ice will quickly melt and vaporize, providing steam.

Foil Liners

While parchment is still used in bakeries and restaurant kitchens to line baking sheets and cake pans, the foil you already have on hand will work very well to the same end. Like baker's parchment, it aids in unmolding delicate cakes and chilled desserts, and afterward you won't have to scrub the pan.

Liners For Baking Sheets

To line a baking sheet, simply lay a large piece of foil on the sheet. (There's no need to secure it; the weight of the food will keep it in place.) After toasting nuts or brown rice on a foil-lined sheet, the liner can be shaped into a cone for funneling every morsel into a container without spills.

If you bake several batches of cookies with only one baking sheet, spoon the dough for each batch onto a foil liner. After one batch is done, cool the baking sheet by rinsing it in cold water, dry it and lay the next batch and its foil liner on the sheet before returning it to the oven.

Liners for Baking Pans

To smoothly line a baking pan from top to bottom: Invert it and shape a piece of foil over its bottom and sides (1). This creates a form that can be slipped into the pan and gently pressed in place as a seamless liner. Of course, the thinner the pan, the more readily the liner will fit it.

Liners for Round Cake Pans

Most cakes will shrink away from the pan's sides when they're done, but invariably stick to the bottom. Making a foil liner for the bottom of the pan is simple: First, invert the pan and lightly mold a piece of foil over its bottom to mark the circle (1). Then remove the foil and, using scissors, cut just inside the circular impression. If there are oil stains burnt on the pan's bottom, dusting a little cornmeal or flour on the bottom of the pan before inserting the liner will simplify its removal.

1

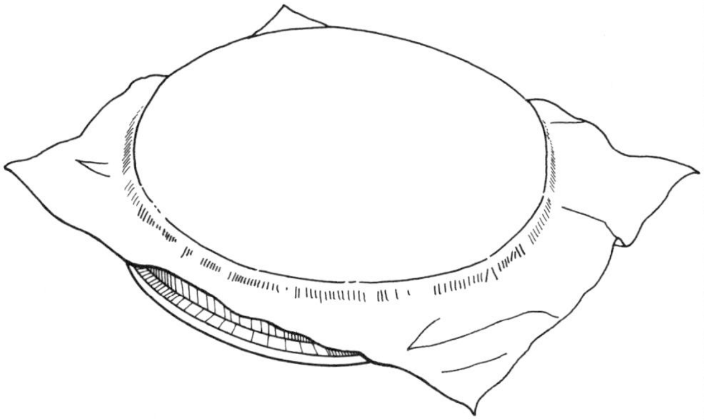

2

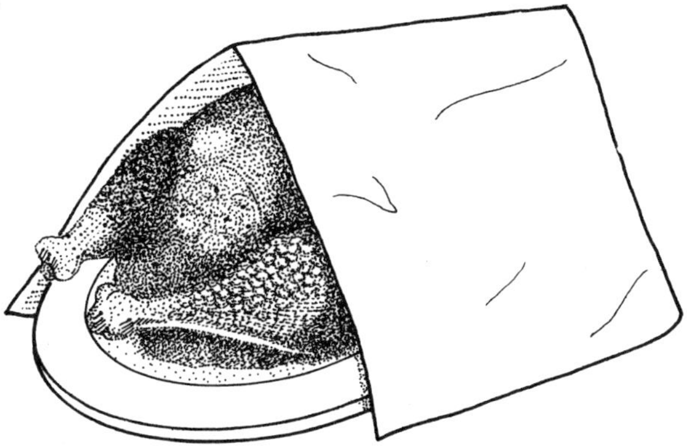

A Foil Tent

After roasted meats and poultry are removed from the oven, they should be transferred to a warm platter to rest before carving. (In fact, they'll continue to cook for several minutes.) To keep the meat warm while it firms up inside and the juices settle, loosely cover the roast with a tent of foil: Crease the center of a large sheet and place it over the roast, leaving the ends open and allowing an inch of space between the meat and the foil (2).

Cook's Tools

for Cooking with Foil

As the owner of such esoterica as an English tongue press and a hinged, star-shaped grill for cooking nothing but fresh sardines, I am in a position to assure you that a great deal of culinary equipment (however alluring it looks) may do little more than add clutter to your cabinets and drawers.

The cook's tools I rely upon daily are eminently practical and on the inexpensive side, and require minimal storage space. Starting with foil products, here are a few that will serve you well with the recipes that follow.

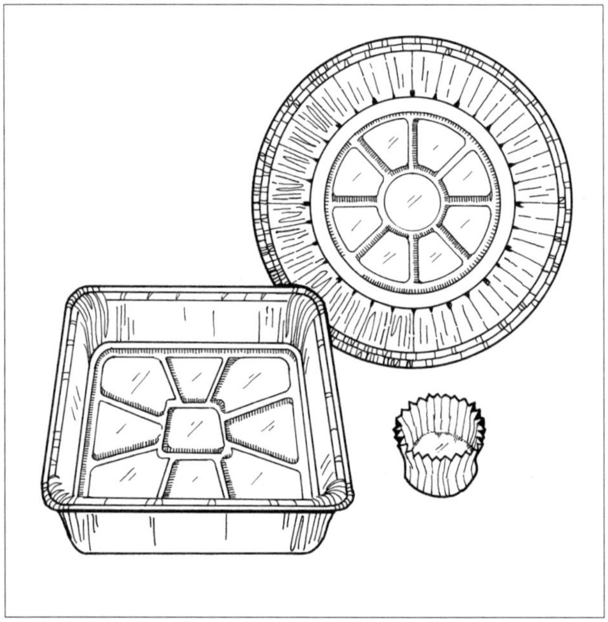

Foil Pans

The inexpensive foil baking pans sold in supermarkets are made from a very durable, lightweight aluminum that is far more rigid than mere foil. Configured in standard pan sizes, the best have ribbed bottoms and crinkled corners that make them very sturdy. While foil pans can never substitute for a good set of metal bakeware, they do come in handy for baked goods that will be transported or frozen. I rely solely on foil pie pans for baking my favorite flat breads *(see pages 93 and 94).*

Aluminum Foil

I use ordinary 12" wide foil to make packets and line most pans and baking sheets. The 18" width is handy for lining large pans and tenting roasts. Reserve thick, heavy-duty foil for lining roasting pans, especially if you make gravy from the pan drippings or use the liner as a sling to lift something as hefty as a crown roast from the pan.

Foil Baking Cups

Unlike paper baking cups that cling tenaciously to muffins (and keep half for themselves), foil cups resist sticking. And because each one stands unaided on a baking sheet, you can bake as many muffins as the sheet will hold and dispense with using (and scrubbing) a muffin tin.

An Olive Oil Sprayer

With a refillable pump sprayer, you can quickly grease a pan or baking sheet. Its fine mist of oil evenly coats the pan's surface—and does so without releasing the chemicals in an aerosol nonstick cooking spray. Made of metal or plastic, the sprayer can also be used for spritzing salads and cooked vegetables with flavorful olive oils.

Ovenware

Your primary consideration in selecting a baking or roasting pan is its size: It should fit inside your oven with two inches to spare all around. This allows hot air to circulate over and around it. A good **baking sheet** (*cookie sheet*) is durable enough that it won't warp and has an angled front edge for a handhold. Having two is a great help when baking batches of cookies in sequence. Sometimes called a *sheet pan* or *jelly-roll pan*, a **shallow baking pan** has a low rim to catch the spills from liquid ingredients.

A **roasting pan** with sides deep enough to contain a roast's juices is the true workhorse of ovenware. The best of them have rigid, comfortable, easy-to-reach handles, and they are sturdy without being too heavy to lift when filled with a roast and a rack. (Foil roasting pans are effective only as liners.)

A nonstick finish is really not necessary for a baking sheet or a baking-roasting pan once you've gotten into the habit of lining it with aluminum foil.

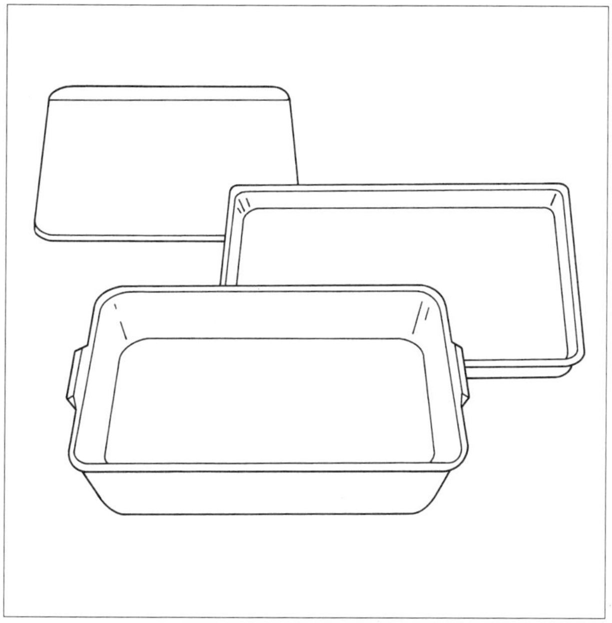

A Roasting Rack

When roasting a whole bird or a large cut of meat, always elevate it on a sturdy rack well above the drippings so air can circulate all around it. Consensus favors a horizontal rack that cradles the roast. The more surface area to the rack, the better it crisps the skin touching the metal.

Standard Baking Pans

As a writer of recipes, I appreciate the fact that the manufacturers of cookware seldom stray too far from the standard dimensions of loaf and cake pans used by so many generations of cooks. Metal and glass **loaf pans** still measure about 8" by 4" and 2½" deep; **round layer cake pans** are available with diameters of 8" and 9"; and **square baking pans** are 8" and 9" square.

Cooling Racks

Cookies and cakes fresh out of the oven must be allowed to cool on a rack to prevent their bottoms from turning soggy. If you do any baking at all, you'll need several wire racks: an all-purpose, rectangular rack (as large as your countertop will allow) and two 12" diameter cake racks.

Baking Dishes

Oven-safe ceramic and glass bakeware is designed for cooking foods with a high liquid content. (I use a round ceramic bowl with deep sides for rice and lentils cooked in the oven.) Most are sold without covers, a limitation easily remedied with a piece of foil tightly secured to the rim. The best ones are attractive enough to serve from and, when covered with foil, can be used for refrigerating any leftovers. Standard capacities of baking dishes are 1-quart (4 cups), 1½-quart (6 cups) and 2-quart (8 cups).

A Food Processor

By using an electric food processor, you can prep and combine ingredients in no time at all with accuracy, uniformity and efficiency. Cuisinart introduced the original food processor, but today you'll find many well-made models from which to choose. Be sure to select the size that best suits your needs (bigger isn't always better). And if you come to rely on it as much as I do, you'll want to have two work bowls. The extra bowl will allow you to process a second batch of ingredients without stopping to wash the first bowl.

A Meat Thermometer
Many a culinary disaster could be averted by confirming a roast's internal temperature before removing it from the oven. The best meat thermometers are engineered to remain in the meat while it roasts and to be read at a glance. To position the probe, be sure it reaches deep into the meat without touching bone, fat or gristle. Most thermometers are accurate to within two degrees, but it's wise to test them from time to time, and very simple: Point the probe into a pot of boiling water, and be sure it registers close to 212° (the boiling point of water).

A Pepper Grinder
The fragrance and flavor of freshly ground peppercorns bear no resemblance to that of preground pepper. A good pepper mill is essential in the kitchen, and the French-made Perfex is by far the best one available. Compact in size, manually operated and adjustable for a fine or coarse grind, it is constructed of cast aluminum with metal works throughout. A simple pull-out chute on the side simplifies refilling without dismantling.

A Bulb Baster
Configured like an oversized eyedropper, the bulb baster is an extremely versatile kitchen tool. The newest ones are smartly designed to do much more than baste your Thanksgiving turkey. Most come with an assortment of needles and tips, including a nifty flat one for skimming the fat from cooking juices and handily siphoning excess juices from a plate. If its shaft is made of clear plastic, a baster can double as a fat separator, which is a great help in making gravies and pan sauces.

A Fine-Mesh Strainer
If large enough to fit over a pot or mixing bowl, a strainer with a fine metal mesh makes a respectable substitute for a sieve or colander.

A Citrus Zester
The only easy-to-use tool for freeing the flavorful peel of a lemon or orange (its zest) from the bitter white pith is the zester. In fact, that's all a zester can do: scrape away the outermost skin and create elegant, edible threads from it. (When a recipe calls for wide strips of citrus peel for flavoring foods as they cook, I rely on a good potato peeler.)

An Apple Corer-Slicer
Slices of fruit in a pie or tart bake to the same doneness if each one has been cut to the same size. Of course, that's easier said than done without the right tool. The simplicity of a one-piece, hand-held apple corer-slicer only adds to its ingenuity. With one downward push, it cores an apple (or pear) and slices a dozen identical wedges.

A Pastry Brush
Sterilized natural or nylon bristles distinguish the pastry brush from similar paint brushes. This may well be the most inexpensive cook's tool around, but even so, it's surprising how many good cooks do without one. You'll use it again and again for brushing on a glaze or greasing every inch of a baking pan.

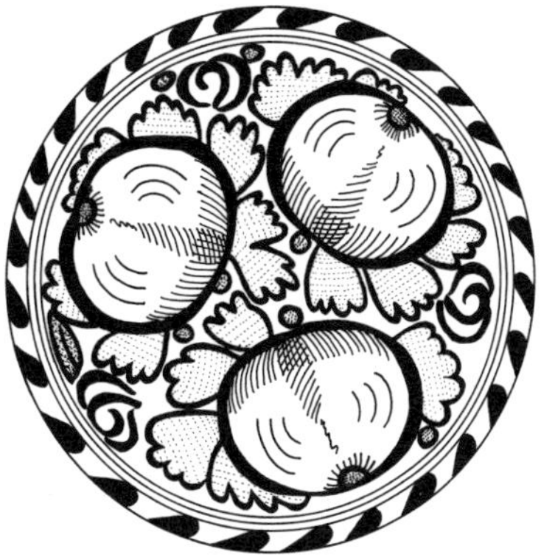

Vegetables

OVER THE PAST TEN YEARS, the produce section of your local supermarket has seen some amazing changes. Such rarities as snow peas, brightly colored bell peppers, slim Asian eggplants, bunches of fresh herbs and giant portabella mushrooms all jostle for the cook's attention.

Of all the happy discoveries to be made when cooking fresh food in foil packets, the way vegetables turn out can be the most rewarding. Flavors are concentrated and heightened; textures are everything they should be; and vitamins are preserved. Flash-roasting vegetables on a foil-lined pan has its rewards as well: Their sugars caramelize to lend a natural sweetness to the finished dish.

Another advantage to cooking vegetables with foil lies in the little attention required. They practically cook and clean up after themselves, allowing the cook to concentrate on other tasks. That's not quite the same as having a sous-chef at your beck and call, but it does help.

It has been said before, but bears repeating: The fresher the ingredients you cook with, the better the results. European cooks visit their greengrocers daily and take home fruits and vegetables at the peak of freshness. Look and ask for the best, and you'll taste the difference.

Buttered Asparagus

An Appetizer or Side Dish

Buttered Asparagus
one serving

- **1 tablespoon butter,** softened
- **6 asparagus**
- **Salt**
- **1 lemon wedge**

An elegant, accommodating vegetable, asparagus goes well with chicken and almost any fish or meat. This recipe proves that you really don't need a fancy asparagus steamer with a wire basket inside "to boil the bottoms and steam the tips," plus yet another saucepan for melting butter as a sauce. With the asparagus and butter steaming together inside a foil packet, their flavors are concentrated.

Preheat the oven to 425°.

For each serving, smear the center area of a 16" length of foil with the butter.

Snap the woody end off each asparagus spear (they'll easily break just below the tender part). Align the spears on a cutting board and, with a knife, evenly trim the bottoms. Then place the spears on the buttered foil, to one side of its center. Season them with salt to taste.

Fold the foil over the asparagus; then fold and tightly crimp the edges together to form a D-shaped packet.

Transfer the packet to a baking sheet, and bake for 12 minutes.

On a dinner plate, slit open the packet's straight side and withdraw the foil, leaving the buttered asparagus on the plate.

Serve with the lemon wedge on the side, for squeezing a little juice on the asparagus at the table.

Note: *To ensure that you're getting the freshest asparagus, look for tightly furled buds and firm stalks. Otherwise, they're really not worth buying or cooking.*

Roasted Asparagus

An Appetizer or Side Dish

Roasted Asparagus
two servings

- **1 tablespoon olive oil**
- **12 asparagus**
- **Salt**

When roasted, asparagus makes a wonderful appetizer or side dish. Top with shavings of a good imported Parmesan cheese or a squeeze of lemon juice. Any leftovers will be delicious served cold with a sprinkling of balsamic vinegar.

Preheat the oven to 425°.

Line a shallow baking pan with foil, and smear its center area with the olive oil.

Snap the woody end off each asparagus spear (they'll easily break just below the tender part). Align the spears on a cutting board, and evenly trim the bottoms. Transfer each one to the foil liner, and roll it over to coat with oil. Arrange them so they don't touch each other. Season with salt to taste.

For medium-thick asparagus, roast for 15 minutes, turning the spears over with tongs after the first ten minutes so both sides can brown slightly. (If using very slender spears, reduce the roasting time to ten minutes and turn them after seven minutes.)

Transfer to a serving platter or dinner plates.

Note: *While roasted asparagus can be enjoyed as an appetizer or side dish, it can also add flavor and interest as an ingredient in other recipes.* *See Asparagus Risotto, page 42.*

Crispy Eggplant Slices
An Appetizer or Side Dish

Crispy Eggplant Slices
four servings (16 slices)

- **2 eggs,** beaten
- **1 cup soft white bread crumbs** *(see page 122)*
- **½ cup grated imported Parmesan**
- **1 medium eggplant** (about 1 pound)
- **Salt and pepper**
- **Olive oil spray**

For this recipe, be sure to select oblong rather than round eggplants. Once they've cooked, slice them in quarters for an irresistible hot appetizer, or serve them whole as a side dish. (Even people who think they loathe eggplant gobble these down and look around for more.) Because the slices aren't soaked in oil, as in so many traditional recipes, they won't be ruinous to your waistline.

Preheat the oven to 425°, and line a shallow baking pan with foil.

Place the beaten eggs in a shallow bowl. Combine the bread crumbs and Parmesan on a plate.

Using a vegetable peeler, peel the eggplant, then cut it crosswise into ½" thick slices.

Dip each slice in the beaten eggs to coat both sides, and then in the crumb mixture, covering both sides and the edge.

Arrange the breaded slices on the pan, and season with salt and pepper to taste. Generously spray them with the olive oil (or drizzle less generously). Then turn each slice over and repeat.

Bake for ten minutes. Remove the pan from the oven and, with a metal spatula, carefully turn each slice over. Return to the oven and bake for another five to eight minutes, until golden and crispy.

Transfer to a serving platter.

Note: *Most eggplant recipes instruct the cook to sprinkle the slices with salt "to remove the bitterness and excess moisture," but when you select firm young eggplants, that won't be necessary. And if long, slim Asian eggplants are available, you can even dispense with peeling.*

Zucchini Squash

Two Appetizers

Almond-Zucchini Appetizer
four servings

- **2 medium zucchini** (10 ounces total), sliced on the diagonal ½" thick
- **1 egg**
- **½ teaspoon chopped fresh oregano** (or ¼ teaspoon dried)
- **½ cup sliced almonds,** finely chopped
- **Salt and pepper**
- **Olive oil spray**

Asian Zucchini Appetizer
two servings

- **1 medium zucchini** (5 ounces), sliced on the diagonal ½" thick
- **1 tablespoon mild vegetable oil**
- **1 teaspoon Asian sesame oil**
- **1 teaspoon sesame seeds**
- **Salt**

My friend Chuck Williams is famous for his more than 100 recipes for cooking zucchini. At the top of my own far shorter list are these hors d'oeuvres, which will whet any appetite.

Almond-Zucchini Appetizer

Preheat the oven to 425°, and line a baking sheet with foil.

Pat the zucchini slices dry with paper towels.

In a shallow bowl, beat the egg; then stir in the oregano. Pour the almonds into another bowl.

Dip each zucchini slice in the beaten egg to coat both sides, and then in the almonds. Arrange the slices on the foil, season with salt and pepper, and generously spray both sides with olive oil.

Bake for eight minutes, then turn each slice over and bake for five minutes more, until the almonds are golden.

Let them cool slightly on paper towels before serving warm.

Asian Zucchini Appetizer

Preheat the oven to 425°, and line a baking sheet with foil.

Pat the zucchini slices dry with paper towels. Place them in a bowl, and drizzle with the vegetable oil and sesame oil, stirring until well coated. Arrange the slices on the foil, and sprinkle each side with the sesame seeds.

Bake for eight minutes, then turn each slice over and bake for five minutes more. Let them cool slightly on paper towels, and season lightly with salt before serving warm.

Note: *Both of these appetizers may be served as a side dish. (Also, see the recipe for Roasted Zucchini on page 48.)*

Bell Pepper Soup
with Red and Yellow Bell Peppers

Bell Pepper Soup
four servings

- **2 red bell peppers**
- **2 yellow bell peppers**
- **2 medium russet potatoes** (12 ounces total), peeled and chopped
- **2 large garlic cloves,** finely chopped
- **3 cups broth** (vegetable or chicken)
- **Salt**
- **2 cups milk** (whole or low-fat)
- **Pepper** (preferably fresh ground)
- **4 tablespoons plain yogurt** (or sour cream), at room temperature

This hearty soup is an intense, brilliant orange color. A watercolor by San Francisco artist Mark Adams was its inspiration; when he sampled it, he said approvingly, "Ah, this is gutsy," and finished every speck of it. I couldn't have been more delighted. (No doubt you're wondering where foil comes into play with a soup recipe: The peppers are roasted on foil.)

Oven roast and peel the bell peppers. *(See Techniques, page 22.)*

Place the potatoes and garlic in a saucepan with the broth and a pinch of salt. Boil gently until the potatoes are tender, about 15 minutes. With a fork or potato masher, mash the potato and garlic into the liquid until smooth.

Using a food processor, puree the bell peppers. Then add the puree to the potato mixture. Stir in the milk and season with salt and pepper to taste. Heat through, stirring constantly.

Transfer the soup to bowls, and garnish each serving with a spoonful of yogurt.

Note: *Fresh garlic is always available, thanks to staggered harvests worldwide, and should be selected for its all-around firmness and absence of bruises. Garlic will keep for months, depending on its freshness when purchased and the kitchen's heat and humidity. Store garlic in an open container in a cool, dark, airy location. (Refrigeration is not recommended.)*

Red and Yellow Bell Peppers

Techniques

Bell peppers, sometimes known as pimientos, are the fruit of a plant that originated in Latin America; but unlike their fiery cousin the chili, ripe red and yellow bell peppers have a sweet, mellow taste.

The green ones are harvested well before they've ripened. You might expect them to mature to yellow or red and develop their full flavor on a windowsill, as tomatoes do, but it isn't so with bell peppers. They remain rather astringent and are, to my mind at least, inedible when served raw and unpeeled in salads.

The thin, papery skin of bell peppers (regardless of their color) is notoriously indigestible. Removing it is imperative—and actually quite easy if the peppers are roasted or broiled first. Once peeled, bell peppers can then be added to salads and many other dishes for flavor as well as color.

Roasting Technique

Halve each bell pepper, discarding the seeds and pith. Line a shallow baking pan with foil. Spray the foil with olive oil and place the pepper halves on it, skin side up.

Roast at 350° for 30 minutes. The peppers' skin will puff up, and the underside will begin to caramelize. Remove the pan from the oven, cover it with a sheet of foil, and let the peppers rest for ten minutes. (The steam that collects will help to separate the skin from the pulp.)

Peel off the papery skins, and place the peppers in a bowl. Cover and refrigerate for use later.

Broiling Technique

Line the broiler pan with foil, and preheat the broiler.

Cut each bell pepper into quarters, discarding the core, seeds and pith. Trim the curved ends if necessary to make sure each piece lies flat, exposing as much of its skin as possible to the direct heat above. Arrange the pieces, skin side up, in one layer on the foil liner.

Broil about ten minutes, until the skins begin to blacken and blister. Remove the pan, cover it with a second sheet of foil, and let the peppers rest for ten minutes.

Peel off the papery skins, and place the peppers in a bowl. Cover and refrigerate for use later.

Note: *When selecting bell peppers, look for firm, unspotted ones with smooth, shiny skins.*

Roasted Bell Peppers

Appetizer & Diced Vegetable Salad

Bell Pepper Appetizer
two servings

- **1 red bell pepper**
- **1 yellow bell pepper**
- **Salt and pepper**
- **Olive oil spray**
- **Balsamic vinegar**

Diced Vegetable Salad
four servings

- **1 red bell pepper**
- **2 cucumbers**
- **4 ripe tomatoes**
- **6 green onions** (including pale green leaves)
- **½ cup shredded cilantro leaves**
- **½ cup shredded basil leaves**
- **Salt and pepper**
- **2 tablespoons white wine vinegar**

Bell Pepper Appetizer

A quintessential Mediterranean dish, colorful roasted bell peppers are delicious with black olives and crusty bread, or as a salad ingredient.

Roast and peel the bell peppers *(see Techniques, page 22)*, then cut them into wide strips. In a serving dish, season them lightly with salt and pepper. Then lightly spray them with olive oil, and sprinkle with a few drops of balsamic vinegar. Serve at room temperature.

Diced Vegetable Salad

The origin of this herb-scented salad is the Middle East. It makes a refreshing buffet dish—with the added benefit of containing no oil.

Roast and peel the bell pepper *(see Techniques, page 22)*, then dice it. Peel, seed and dice the cucumbers and tomatoes. Chop the onions.

In a serving bowl, combine the bell pepper, cucumbers, tomatoes, onions, cilantro and basil.

Season with salt and pepper, sprinkle with the vinegar, and mix gently before serving.

Note: *To peel a tomato, cut a cross in its base, and immerse the tomato in boiling water for ten seconds. With a slotted spoon, transfer it to a bowl of cold water for ten seconds, then drain. The skin can then be easily peeled by hand from the cuts in the base. To remove the seeds, slice the peeled tomato in half around its equator and scoop the seeds out with a teaspoon.*

Oven-Steamed Broccoli

Florets & Italian-Style Stems

Steamed Broccoli Florets
two servings

- **Olive oil spray**
- **1 cup broccoli florets** (from 2 stalks)
- **Salt and pepper**
- **½ cup water**

Italian-Style Broccoli Stems
two servings

- **1 tablespoon olive oil**
- **1 cup broccoli stem sticks** (from 2 stalks)
- **1 garlic clove,** sliced very thin
- **Salt and pepper**
- **1 ice cube**

Because broccoli florets cook faster than their stems, it makes sense to cook and serve the two separately. (The florets should be cooked when very fresh; the stems may be refrigerated for several days.) Cooking them under foil achieves just the right degree of tender crispness.

Steamed Broccoli Florets

Preheat the oven to 425°.

Spray a baking dish with olive oil, and arrange the florets in it in a single layer. Season with salt and pepper to taste, then add the water. Cover tightly with foil, and bake for 15 minutes.

Carefully remove the foil, releasing the steam; and with a bulb baster, siphon off the remaining water before serving.

Italian-Style Broccoli Stems

Preheat the oven to 425°.

Smear the center area of a 16" length of foil with the olive oil, and roll the broccoli sticks in the oil. Top with the garlic, and season with salt and pepper to taste. Then add the ice cube.

Fold the foil over the broccoli sticks; then fold and tightly crimp the edges together to form a D-shaped packet. Transfer the packet to a baking sheet, and bake for 15 minutes.

Snip open the top of the packet, and spoon out the broccoli.

Note: *To quickly trim the broccoli stems after the florets have been removed, use a paring knife to cut each one into a four-sided column. Then divide it into sticks about ¼" wide and 2" long. The more uniform they are, the better.*

Buttered Baby Carrots

A Side Dish

Buttered Baby Carrots
one serving

- **1 tablespoon butter,** softened
- **4 ounces tiny carrots,** trimmed
- **Salt and pepper**
- **Nutmeg** (preferably fresh ground)
- **1 tablespoon orange juice**

With a little orange juice and nutmeg to augment their natural sweetness, carrots taste wonderful cooked in a foil packet. (When preparing carrots for cooking, keep in mind that their flavor is concentrated toward the large end.)

With a baking sheet in place, preheat the oven to 425°.

In a skillet, heat the butter, add the carrots, and sauté for one minute. Season with salt and pepper to taste, and a generous sprinkling of nutmeg; then stir in the orange juice.

For each serving, transfer the carrots to a 16" length of foil, placing them to one side of its center.

Fold the foil over the carrots; then fold and tightly crimp the edges together to form a D-shaped packet. Transfer the packet to the hot baking sheet, and bake for 15 minutes.

On a dinner plate, slit open the packet's straight side and withdraw the foil, leaving the carrots and their sauce on the plate.

Note: *If you can't find immature carrots 1½" to 2" long, peel slender full-size ones and cut them into 1½" lengths. Then, with a paring knife, round the ends of each piece. As an alternative, cut large peeled carrots into matchsticks about ½" wide and 1½" long and reduce the time to ten minutes.*

Roasted Corn

Corn & Black Bean Salad

Roasted Corn
one serving

- **1 very fresh ear of corn**
- **1½ tablespoons butter,** softened
- **Salt**

Corn & Black Bean Salad
four servings

- **½ teaspoon salt**
- **1½ tablespoons red wine vinegar**
- **6 tablespoons olive oil**
- **Pepper**
- **2 cups corn kernels** (from 4 to 5 ears of roasted corn)
- **1 red bell pepper,** broiled, peeled and chopped *(see Techniques, page 22)*
- **1 cup black beans** (cooked or canned), drained
- **4 green onions** (including pale green leaves), chopped
- **20 green olives,** pitted and sliced
- **¼ cup chopped cilantro**

Fresh corn on the cob is a summertime treat that, once experienced, is never forgotten. Its kernels are sweet and buttery even before you've buttered them. Not surprisingly, a salad of freshly roasted corn tastes wonderful and is particularly good in combination with black beans, roasted red bell peppers and sprightly cilantro leaves.

Roasted Corn

Preheat the oven to 400°.

Husk the ear of corn, and remove its silk.

For each serving, smear the center of a 12" length of foil with half the softened butter. Place a single ear of corn on the foil, and loosely fold it over the corn, crimping the edges tightly together to form an oblong packet.

Place the packet on a baking sheet, and bake for 25 minutes.

On a dinner plate, slit open the packet and withdraw the foil, leaving the corn on the plate.

Smear the corn with the remaining butter, and season with salt before serving.

Corn & Black Bean Salad

Cut the kernels from the corn over a bowl to conserve its sweet juices. Then in a large bowl, dissolve the salt in the vinegar and whisk in the olive oil and pepper, to taste. Add the corn, broiled bell pepper, beans, green onions, olives and cilantro. Taste for seasoning. Cover and refrigerate for up to three hours before serving.

Note: *Because the sugar in young corn converts to starch as it matures, use it without delay, while it's still sweet. To remove the kernels, stand the cob upright at a slight angle on a cutting board, and scrape the kernels off with a knife, reaching as close to the hard cob as possible. Then scrape the cob once more to release the last bit of juice.*

Quick-Baked Lentils
and Lentil Salad

Quick-Baked Lentils
two servings (1½ cups)

- **Olive oil spray**
- **2 tablespoons finely chopped shallot** (or onion)
- **Small bay leaf**
- **½ cup lentils,** rinsed
- **1¼ cups boiling water**
- **Salt and pepper**

Lentil Salad
two servings

- **4 tablespoons olive oil**
- **1½ tablespoons sherry vinegar**
- **¼ cup minced green onions** (including pale green leaves)
- **2 small ribs celery,** minced
- **1½ cups cooked lentils** (warm), drained
- **Salt and pepper**
- **3 tablespoons chopped cilantro**

One of the first crops to be cultivated, lentils have been served as a food for at least 8,000 years. Green lentils imported from France have a distinctive flavor and texture, which may account for the prevalence of lentil soups and casseroles on European dinner tables. The difference makes green lentils well worth shopping for. Like beans and peas, lentils are a legume; but unlike dried beans and peas, dried lentils don't require an overnight soaking.

Quick-Baked Lentils

Preheat the oven to 350°.

Spray the interior of a one-quart (four-cup) oven-safe bowl with olive oil. (If doubling the quantity, be sure to use a large bowl since lentils tend to froth as they cook.)

Add the shallot, bay leaf and lentils. Then pour in the boiling water, and tightly cover the bowl with foil.

Bake for 35 minutes, or until tender to the bite. Discard the bay leaf, and season with salt and pepper before serving.

Lentil Salad

In a bowl, mix the olive oil, vinegar, onions and celery. Toss with the warm lentils, and season with salt and pepper to taste. Let cool, and sprinkle with the cilantro before serving.

Note: *Imported green lentils are available from natural-foods stores. Brown domestic lentils are fine, but can taste a bit floury. Pretty little coral-colored lentils are best reserved for soups, since they tend to break up as they cook. Before cooking lentils, be sure to rinse them and discard any small stones.*

Stuffed Portabella Mushroom

and Portabella "Pizza" Appetizer

Stuffed Portabella Mushroom
one serving

- **1 portabella mushroom** (5 to 6 ounces)
- **1½ tablespoons olive oil**
- **1 large shallot,** finely chopped
- **¼ cup finely chopped celery**
- **¼ cup soft white bread crumbs** *(see page 122)*
- **1 slice prosciutto** (1 ounce), chopped
- **Salt and pepper**
- **1 tablespoon grated imported Parmesan**

Portabella "Pizza" Appetizer
one serving

Preheat the oven to 400°. For each serving, spray one portabella mushroom (stem removed) on both sides with olive oil, and place it on a foil-lined baking sheet. Season it with salt, pepper and dried oregano. Then top with thin tomato slices, strips of roasted bell pepper *(see Techniques, page 22),* pitted black olives and grated Parmesan. Bake for ten minutes.

Unlike mild, white button mushrooms, large flat portabellas have an almost meaty taste and a firm, chewy texture. Filled with this tasty stuffing, a good-size portabella (4" diameter) becomes a meal in itself. What I call Portabella Pizza—a medium-large mushroom (3" diameter) with typical pizza toppings—makes a delicious appetizer.

With a baking sheet in place, preheat the oven to 400°.

Remove the mushroom's stem. Discard its gritty-looking end, and finely chop the remaining part of the stem.

Heat one tablespoon of the olive oil in a skillet. Add the chopped mushroom stem, shallot and celery. Cook over medium heat, stirring often, for five minutes, until softened. Then stir in the bread crumbs and prosciutto. Season with salt and pepper to taste.

For each serving, smear the center area of a 14" length of foil with the remaining olive oil. Place the mushroom cap to one side of the center, and fill it with the stuffing. Top with the grated Parmesan.

Fold the foil over the mushroom; then fold and tightly crimp the edges together to form a D-shaped packet. Transfer the packet to the hot baking sheet, and bake for 15 minutes.

Over a dinner plate, slit open the packet's straight side and withdraw the foil, leaving the stuffed mushroom on the plate.

Note: *Refrigerate mushrooms in a paper bag until they're used. (Stored in plastic, they develop soft spots.) Mushrooms absorb moisture, so they shouldn't be soaked in water. A wipe with a damp paper towel is sufficient to clean them. And with so much flavor concentrated in their skin, peeling is not recommended.*

Garlic-Stuffed Potatoes

A Side Dish

Garlic-Stuffed Potatoes
four servings

- **1 whole head fresh garlic**
- **2 large russet potatoes** (8 ounces each)
- **Salt and white pepper**
- **1 tablespoon olive oil**
- **2 to 3 tablespoons milk** (whole or low-fat)
- **½ tablespoon cold butter,** cut up

It's naturally an Irish proverb that goes "'Tis the potato that's the queen of the garden." While the Irish were somewhat less thrilled by garlic, the flavors of potatoes and roasted garlic complement one another perfectly. The garlic's pungent taste becomes mellow and buttery. (Be sure to use the plumpest, firmest head of garlic you can find.)

With a baking sheet in place, preheat the oven to 375°.

Remove the garlic head's loose skins, and cut off the top third to expose the raw cloves. Wrap the garlic head in a sheet of foil (leaving a little air space inside), and tightly crimp the edges.

Place the potatoes and foil-wrapped garlic on the hot baking sheet, and bake one hour, until the potatoes and the garlic are soft.

Cut the potatoes in half lengthwise. Scoop out the centers, leaving ¼" thick shells. Set aside the shells, and reserve the potato pulp in a mixing bowl.

Unwrap the garlic and pick out the cloves with the tip of a knife, letting them fall into the bowl with the potatoes. Season with salt and pepper, add the olive oil, and mash with a fork or potato masher until very smooth. (Never use a food processor for mashing potatoes; they will turn to glue.)

Stir in enough milk to give the mashed potato pulp a creamy consistency, then spoon it back into the potato shells. Score the tops with a fork, and dot with butter. Return the potatoes to the oven for a few minutes to heat through, or place them under a preheated broiler long enough to form a golden crust.

Note: *If any of these savory potato halves should be left over, top them with thinly sliced Swiss cheese and reheat them on a foil-lined baking sheet the next day. With a green salad and perhaps a glass of red wine, they make a simple, delicious lunch.*

Herbed New Potatoes

A Side Dish

Herbed New Potatoes
one serving

- **4 to 6 small potatoes** (4 ounces total), red or white
- **2 teaspoons olive oil**
- **½ teaspoon chopped fresh thyme** (or rosemary or oregano), or ¼ teaspoon dried
- **Salt and pepper**

Tiny, round new potatoes aren't really "new," they're simply harvested before they mature. As a result, their skins have a smooth texture, and they retain their shape well when cooked. Rather surprisingly, the cut sides of the potatoes brown nicely inside a foil packet, so you end up with the appetizing look of fried potatoes without the disadvantages of food saturated with oil.

With a baking sheet in place, preheat the oven to 425°.

Cut the potatoes in half.

For each serving, smear the center area of a 16" length of foil with the olive oil. Arrange the potatoes on it, cut sides down, to one side of its center. Season lightly with salt and pepper, and sprinkle with the thyme.

Fold the foil over the potatoes; then fold and tightly crimp the edges together to form a D-shaped packet. Transfer the packet to the hot baking sheet, and bake for 25 minutes.

On a dinner plate, slit open the packet's straight side and withdraw the foil, leaving the potatoes on the plate.

Note: *If you're cooking two servings, double the ingredients and bake them in one packet.*

Oven-Fried Potato Wedges

A Side Dish

Oven-Fried Potato Wedges
one serving

- **Olive oil spray**
- **1 large russet potato** (8 ounces), peeled
- **Salt**
- **½ teaspoon dried rosemary** (or thyme or oregano)

A lot like french fries, but without the fat, these delectable potato wedges are golden brown and crispy on the outside and soft inside. Rosemary, thyme or oregano (in this case dried is better than fresh) adds all the flavor needed for a truly versatile side dish with steak, chops or chicken.

Preheat the oven to 425°.

Line a shallow baking pan with foil, and generously spray it with olive oil.

Cut the potato into eight long wedges of equal size. Dry them thoroughly with paper towels to promote browning.

Place each wedge on the foil liner, and roll it in the oil to coat its surface. Then arrange them (without touching one another) on the foil.

Season with salt to taste, and sprinkle with the dried rosemary.

Bake for ten minutes; then turn the wedges over, and bake for another ten minutes.

Note: *When an unpeeled potato is baked in a tight foil wrapper, its natural moisture isn't released as steam. That's why the inside of the potato turns out soggy instead of fluffy.*

Buttered Radishes

A Side Dish

Buttered Radishes
one serving

- **6 medium radishes** (4 ounces total)
- **1 tablespoon butter**
- **1 shallot, chopped**
- **Salt and white pepper**

Radishes are most often served raw—sliced in a salad or used as a colorful garnish. But when baked in foil, radishes turn pale pink and develop a mellow rather than peppery taste—somewhat like a delectable little turnip. It's a flavor that goes particularly well with roast pork, duck or lamb. (Two servings can be baked in one packet.)

With a baking sheet in place, preheat the oven to 425°.

Wash and trim the radishes, and cut larger ones in half through their equator.

In a small skillet, heat the butter, add the shallot, and sauté for one minute. Then add the radishes, and roll them around to coat with butter. Season with salt and pepper to taste.

Transfer the radishes and shallots to a 16" length of foil, to one side of its center.

Fold the foil over the radishes; then fold and tightly crimp the edges together to form a D-shaped packet. Transfer the packet to the hot baking sheet, and bake for 15 minutes.

On a dinner plate, slit open the packet's straight side and withdraw the foil, leaving the buttered radishes on the plate.

Note: *When shopping for radishes, remember that the smaller, less mature ones offer the most flavor. Give them a gentle squeeze to be sure they're firm; and if any leaves are still attached, they should be crisp and green.*

Zucchini Provençal
A Side Dish

Zucchini Provençal
four servings

- **Olive oil spray**
- **2 tablespoons olive oil**
- **½ medium onion,** chopped
- **2 large garlic cloves,** finely chopped
- **2 zucchini** (10 ounces total), diced
- **2 ripe tomatoes,** peeled, seeded and diced
- **½ red bell pepper,** broiled, peeled and diced *(see Techniques, page 22)*
- **¼ cup chopped fresh basil**
- **Salt and pepper**

Zucchini is an amazingly versatile squash. When combined with other vegetables and garlic, the result is a variation on the classic French ratatouille that makes a colorful side dish.

Preheat the oven to 375°.

Spray the interior of a one-quart (four-cup) oven-safe bowl with olive oil.

In a skillet, heat one tablespoon of the olive oil, and sauté the onion and garlic until softened but not browned.

Then, in the bowl, mix the onion and garlic with the zucchini, tomatoes, bell pepper and basil. Sprinkle with the remaining olive oil, and season with salt and pepper to taste.

Tightly cover the bowl with foil, and bake for 30 minutes; then bake uncovered for ten minutes to reduce and concentrate the juices.

Note: *Look for zucchini that are fairly small with tight, shiny skins. Before chopping fresh basil, lightly spray the leaves with olive oil, and the chopped leaves will be less apt to darken around the edges.*

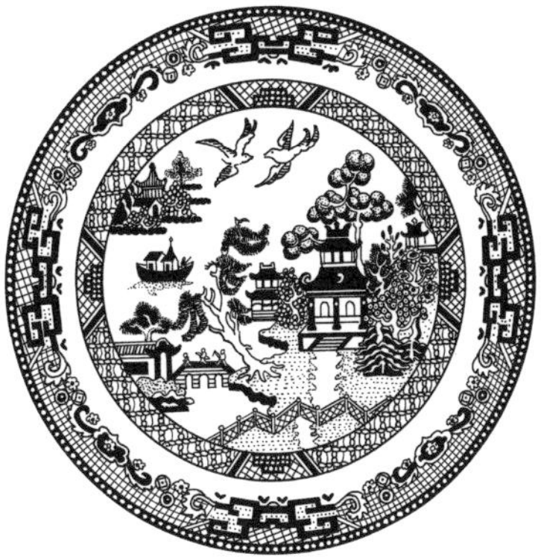

Rice

For a majority of our planet's population, rice is the staple grain. In its various forms, more rice is consumed than any other food. Because we Westerners cannot live without bread (much less on bread alone), we've developed our own flavorful recipes for rice. In Spain, it's paella; in Italy, risotto; in England, rice pudding; and in America, rice-and-bean dishes.

Perhaps unexpectedly, aluminum foil can be your best friend when it comes to cooking rice. Long-grain white rice bakes to perfection in a bowl tightly sealed with foil. And if you're heating the oven anyway, it's easy enough to cook a side dish of rice alongside the main course.

I follow this same technique for rice pilaf dishes after sautéing the rice with chopped onion and adding aromatics, and for rich brown rice after toasting the grains in a foil-lined pan.

Most amazing of all, soul-satisfying Italian risotto can be made very successfully in the oven under foil, which eliminates standing over a hot stove and stirring for half an hour. If this sounds heretical, I should point out that the traditional stand-and-stir method originated in Italy's Lombardy region, and in the Piedmont and Veneto, some very fine cooks also prefer to make their creamy risotto covered and unattended.

Rice Salad
with Zucchini & Smoked Ham

Zucchini and Rice Salad
four servings

- **3 cups warm white rice** *(see page 39)*
- **Salt and pepper**
- **1 tablespoon sherry vinegar**
- **⅓ cup plus 1 tablespoon olive oil**
- **1 teaspoon Dijon mustard**
- **2 medium zucchini** (10 ounces total)
- **2 green onions** (including pale green leaves), finely chopped
- **1 red or yellow bell pepper,** broiled, peeled and diced *(see Techniques, page 22)*
- **2 ounces smoked ham,** diced

Grain salads make a good light meal in summer as well as the ideal side dish for a buffet dinner. In this recipe, rice flavored and colored with turmeric provides a neutral background for the flavors of bell peppers, zucchini and smoked ham.

Start by cooking the rice (doubling the recipe for White Rice on page 39 and adding ½ teaspoon of turmeric with the butter).

In a small bowl, make the dressing by dissolving ¼ teaspoon of salt in the vinegar. Then whisk in ⅓ cup of olive oil, the mustard and pepper to taste. Set the dressing aside.

With a foil-lined baking sheet in place, preheat the oven to 425°.

Cut the zucchini on the diagonal into slices ½" thick, and pat them dry with paper towels.

In a large bowl, toss the zucchini slices with one tablespoon of olive oil. Arrange them on the hot, foil-lined baking sheet, and bake for eight minutes. Then turn the pieces over, and bake for five minutes more, until they turn a rich golden brown.

Remove the zucchini, and cut each slice into quarters. Lightly season them with salt.

Stir the dressing into the warm rice. Then gently stir in the zucchini, green onions, bell pepper and ham. Toss gently and taste for seasoning. Serve warm or at room temperature.

Note: *The secret to a good rice salad is to add the dressing while the rice is still warm, when it will be more readily absorbed.*

Easy Oven Rice

Technique

1½-cup yield 1-qt. bowl	3-cup yield 1½-qt. bowl	6-cup yield 2½-qt. bowl
½ cup rice	1 cup rice	2 cups rice
1 cup liquid	2 cups liquid	3½ cups liquid
½ Tbsp. butter or oil	1 Tbsp. butter or oil	1½ Tbsp. butter or oil
¼ tsp. salt	½ tsp. salt	1 tsp. salt
18 minutes	18 minutes	18 minutes

Cooking rice under foil in the oven ensures that the grains remain separate and come out tender and fluffy every time.

This technique for cooking long-grain white rice is quick and easy, as illustrated below. And by adjusting the oven temperature and baking time, you can use the same basic procedure to prepare flavorful rice pilafs (18 minutes), creamy Italian risotto (20 minutes), hearty brown rice (40 minutes) and savory wild rice (60 minutes).

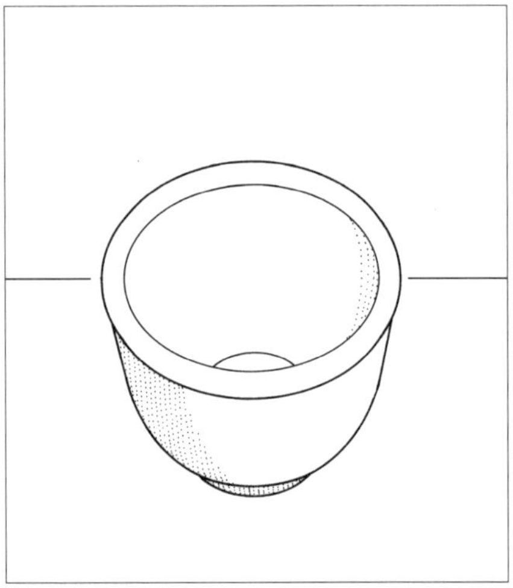

Step 1 Use an oven-safe bowl (glass or ceramic) with a pronounced rim on which to secure the foil. Lightly spray its interior with olive oil.

Note: *The oven must be preheated to 425°.*

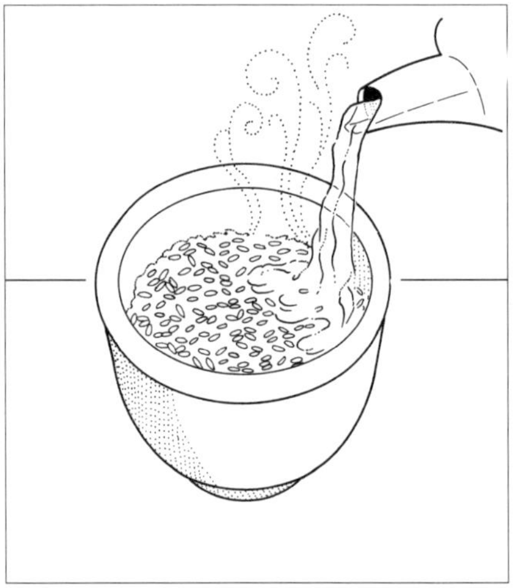

Step 2 Add the white rice, the butter or oil, and the salt (unless you're using a salted broth). Then pour in the boiling water or broth.

Note: *The liquid must be heated to boiling.*

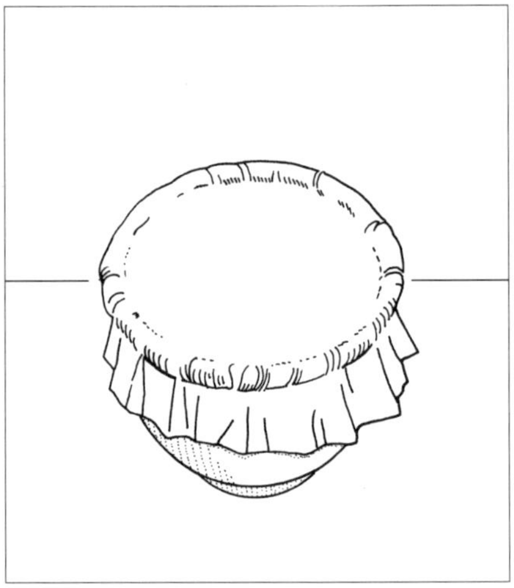

Step 3 Tightly cover the bowl with foil, and transfer it to the oven. After the rice has baked 18 minutes, take the bowl from the oven, and carefully remove the foil, releasing the hot steam. Fluff with a fork before serving.

Easy Oven Rice

Recipes

Easy Oven Rice (White Rice)
two servings (1½ cups)

- **Olive oil spray**
- **½ cup long-grain white rice**
- **½ tablespoon butter** (or vegetable oil)
- **¼ teaspoon salt**
- **1 cup boiling liquid** (water, chicken broth or vegetable broth)

Spicy Golden Rice

- **1½ cups cooked white rice** *(see above)*
- **1 tablespoon Zante currants,** rinsed and drained
- **¼ teaspoon ground cumin**
- **¼ teaspoon ground turmeric**

Almond Rice

- **1½ cups cooked white rice** *(see above)*
- **Olive oil spray**
- **¼ cup sliced almonds**

Basil-Flavored Rice

- **1½ cups cooked white rice** *(see above)*
- **2 tablespoons chopped fresh basil**

Easy Oven Rice (White Rice)

Preheat the oven to 425°.

Spray the interior of a one-quart (four-cup) oven-safe bowl with olive oil. Then add the rice, butter and salt (unless you're using a salted broth as the liquid).

Pour in the boiling liquid, and tightly cover the bowl with foil. Bake for 18 minutes.

Carefully remove the foil, and fluff the rice with a fork before serving. (If the rice is too moist, leave the bowl uncovered in the hot oven for two to three minutes more.)

Spicy Golden Rice

Follow the recipe for Easy Oven Rice. Add the currants, cumin and turmeric with the butter.

Almond Rice

Follow the recipe for Easy Oven Rice. Meanwhile, in a skillet sprayed with a little olive oil, heat the almonds and stir until golden, one to two minutes. Scatter over the cooked rice before serving.

Basil-Flavored Rice

Follow the recipe for Easy Oven Rice. Stir the basil into the cooked rice just before serving.

Note: *Dry rice expands to three times its volume when cooked. 1½ cups of cooked rice will provide two generous servings. For more than two servings, use the chart on page 38 to determine the size of the bowl and the proportions of the basic ingredients. Then increase any additional ingredients accordingly.*

Rice Pilaf

A Side Dish

Rice Pilaf
two servings

- **1 tablespoon olive oil**
- **1 tablespoon minced shallot** (or onion)
- **½ cup long-grain white rice**
- **1 teaspoon grated lemon zest**
- **¼ teaspoon salt** (if broth is unsalted)
- **1 cup boiling broth** (chicken or vegetable)
- **1 tablespoon chopped fresh parsley** (or cilantro)
- **2 tablespoons pomegranate seeds** (optional, see *Note*)

A prominent dish on dinner tables in the Middle East, rice pilaf combines any number of savory ingredients and long-grain white rice. With meat, fish or poultry included, it becomes the entire meal; but this lightly seasoned pilaf is intended as a side dish. If pomegranates are in season, by all means scatter the seeds over the pilaf just before it's served. They look like sparkling little jewels and add that sweet-sharp flavor that is theirs alone.

Preheat the oven to 400°.

In a skillet, heat the oil, and add the shallot. Let it simmer for three minutes.

Add the rice and cook for one minute, stirring frequently.

Stir in the lemon zest. If the broth is unsalted, add the salt.

Transfer to a one-quart (four-cup) oven-safe bowl, and add the boiling broth.

Tightly cover the bowl with foil, and bake for 18 minutes.

Carefully remove the foil. (If the rice is too moist, leave the bowl uncovered in the hot oven for two to three minutes more.) Stir in the chopped parsley. Fluff the rice with a fork.

Let it rest uncovered for five minutes before serving. If using pomegranate seeds as a garnish, scatter them over the rice.

Note: *Pomegranates are harvested from early to late autumn. Removing the seeds may prove daunting, unless you first slice off a little of the stem end and make five or six shallow cuts through the skin from top to bottom. Then, using your fingers, pull the fruit apart in sections. If you'll bend each section back, clusters of seeds can be easily plucked from the pith.*

Toasted Brown Rice

A Side Dish

Toasted Brown Rice
two servings

- ½ **cup brown rice** (medium- or long-grain)
- **Olive oil spray**
- **1 tablespoon butter** (or vegetable oil)
- ¼ **teaspoon salt** (if broth is unsalted)
- **1 cup boiling liquid** (water, chicken broth or vegetable broth)

Brown rice, which is simply unpolished white rice, requires longer to cook than white rice. That and its chewy texture may explain why many cooks shy away from this more flavorful variety of rice. But toasting the grains in a foil-lined pan before baking them in a foil-covered bowl transforms brown rice: Instead of becoming gummy, the grains remain separate and tender. Their delicious, nutty taste is worth the extra time.

Preheat the oven to 350°.

Line a shallow baking pan with foil, and spread the rice out on it. Bake for eight minutes—the grains will puff slightly and develop a nutty aroma. Remove them from the oven, and increase the temperature to 400°.

Lightly spray the interior of a one-quart (four-cup) oven-safe bowl with olive oil.

Shape the foil into a funnel and pour the hot rice into the prepared bowl. Add the butter, salt (if the broth is unsalted) and boiling liquid. Tightly cover the bowl with foil, and bake for 40 minutes.

Carefully remove the foil. (If the rice is too moist, leave the bowl uncovered in the hot oven for two to three minutes more.) Fluff the rice with a fork, and let it rest loosely covered with the foil for ten minutes before serving.

Note: *When cooking more than two servings, multiply the ingredients accordingly. See the chart on page 38 for the size of the bowl needed to accommodate larger amounts. The new hybrid brown rices developed in California are well worth seeking out. They have interesting flavors, and their black and mahogany colors give them the earthy appearance of wild rice.*

Asparagus Risotto
and Fried Risotto Pancake

Asparagus Risotto
two servings

- **6 asparagus,** roasted and warm *(see page 18)*
- **1 tablespoon olive oil**
- **2 tablespoons butter**
- **3 tablespoons chopped onion** (or shallot)
- **½ cup arborio or carnaroli rice**
- **Salt and pepper**
- **¼ cup dry white wine**
- **1½ cups boiling broth** (vegetable, chicken or beef)
- **2 tablespoons grated imported Parmesan**

Fried Risotto Pancake
two servings

- **2 large eggs**
- **2 cups cold, cooked risotto**
- **1 tablespoon butter**
- **1 tablespoon grated imported Parmesan**

In Italy, risotto is to the north country what pasta is to the south. As the short, fat grains of arborio or carnaroli rice cook, they absorb lots of flavorful broth, quadrupling in volume to give risotto its distinguishing creaminess. The Italians describe it as risotto all'onda, *that is "risotto with waves."*

While Lombardy cooks stand over the stove, gradually adding the broth and stirring risotto for 30 minutes, cooks in the Piedmont and Veneto are known to cook theirs all at once in a tightly covered pot. This recipe for risotto served as a first course follows the Veneto technique.

The traditional use for leftover risotto is risotto al salto, *or fried risotto. Adding eggs binds the rice into a sort of pancake that remains deliciously creamy beneath its crust. Serve with a green salad, and you'll have a satisfying light dinner for two.*

Asparagus Risotto

Cut the roasted asparagus spears in 1" lengths, and reserve the tips.

Preheat the oven to 350°.

In a skillet, heat the olive oil and one tablespoon of the butter. Add the onion, and simmer for three or four minutes, until soft but not browned.

Add the rice, and stir for one minute, coating the grains well. Season with salt and pepper to taste, using very little salt if the broth is already salted. Add the wine, and let it simmer for two minutes, until the liquid is reduced by half.

Note: *Although excellent served plain, this risotto is flavored with asparagus. Other options include substituting ½ cup of sautéed mushrooms, zucchini chunks, or sliced chicken livers for the asparagus. (In fact, there is no limit to the possibilities.) Don't even think of rinsing the rice before cooking; that would only remove the starches so vital to a successful risotto.*

Transfer to a one-quart (four-cup) oven-safe bowl. Add the boiling broth. Tightly cover the bowl with foil, and bake for 20 minutes.

Carefully remove the foil, and stir the rice (there will be about an inch of broth over it). Test a grain of rice to see that it is almost tender to the bite and not hard in the middle.

Return the uncovered bowl to the oven for another three to five minutes, to finish cooking the rice and reduce a little more of the broth.

Stir in the remaining one tablespoon of butter and the chopped asparagus spears.

Transfer the risotto to a serving bowl, and top it with the asparagus tips and Parmesan.

Fried Risotto Pancake

Lightly beat the eggs in a bowl; then gently stir in the risotto.

In a skillet, heat the butter until it is melted and begins to foam. Add the risotto mixture, and gently press it down with a spatula.

Cook over low heat until the butter bubbles around the edges, about three minutes.

Remove from the heat, and with the spatula, loosen the edges of the pancake so the rice doesn't stick. Cover the pan with a plate, and quickly turn the pan over. Then slide the pancake back into the pan, and let its underside brown for two minutes.

Transfer it to a serving plate, sprinkle with Parmesan, and cut in wedges for serving.

Note: *When cooking more than two servings, multiply the ingredients accordingly. See the chart on page 38 for the size of the bowl for larger amounts. Cold cooked risotto will keep refrigerated for up to two days, so you may want to make a larger quantity than needed in order to have leftovers for the Fried Risotto Pancake.*

Wild Rice Pilaf

A Side Dish

Wild Rice Pilaf
two servings

- **Olive oil spray**
- **1 tablespoon unsalted butter**
- **½ onion,** finely chopped
- **½ cup wild rice**
- **1½ cups chicken broth**
- **Salt and pepper**
- **2 tablespoons chopped pecans,** lightly toasted in a dry skillet

This dark aquatic grass seed, which is native to the Great Lakes region of North America and Canada, has a slightly smoky flavor that further distinguishes it from true rice. Because the extra-long grains are very firm, I prefer cooking them until they begin to split, revealing their white interior. The flavor of plain wild rice is always well-matched with poultry and mushrooms; here the addition of toasted pecans adds a complementary flavor and texture.

Preheat the oven to 350°.

Lightly spray the interior of a one-quart (four-cup) oven-safe bowl with olive oil.

In a skillet, melt the butter over low heat. Add the onion, and cook gently until soft, but not browned, about five minutes.

Stir in the rice. Then add the chicken broth little by little, and bring it to a boil.

Season with ¼ teaspoon of salt (unless the chicken broth is salted) and pepper to taste.

Transfer the rice mixture to the prepared bowl, and tightly cover it with foil. Bake for one hour, or until tender.

Carefully remove the foil. Fluff the rice with a fork, and sprinkle it with the pecans before serving.

Note: *When cooking more than two servings, multiply the ingredients accordingly. See the chart on page 38 for the size of the bowl needed to accommodate larger servings.*

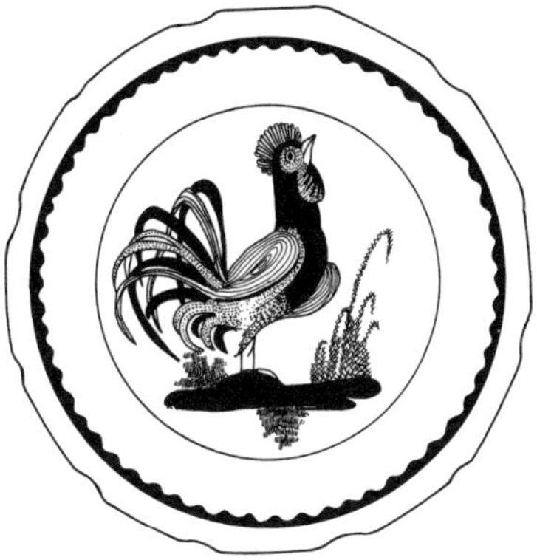

Poultry

BRILLAT-SAVARIN, France's celebrated gastronome, once observed that "...poultry is for the cook what canvas is for the painter," a thought that remains as universally true today as it was in the eighteenth century. In fact, chicken is probably the most commonly eaten meat worldwide, and one would be hard-pressed to name a cuisine (haute or otherwise) without at least one celebrated chicken dish.

The delicate white meat of a chicken or turkey breast lends itself especially well to gentle cooking in a foil packet. There it remains moist and flavorful, absorbing and concentrating the flavors of whatever herbs or vegetables share the packet.

Poultry's dark meat, on the other hand, is at its best when roasted uncovered in the oven. In this case, a foil-lined pan will save a lot of cleanup; and if you're cooking a whole chicken, a piece of foil laid across the breast meat will keep it from drying out while the legs are cooked through.

Tradition almost demands a roast turkey on the Thanksgiving table, and a very good tradition it is. But to keep things interesting, a new stuffing rarely goes amiss. Brown rice with lots of savory sausage, chopped celery, fennel seeds and walnuts makes a tasty addition to the feast.

Chicken Breast Cacciatore

with Prosciutto-Mushroom Stuffing

Chicken Breast Cacciatore
one serving

- **Olive oil spray**
- **1 tablespoon butter**
- **1 large shallot,** finely chopped
- **1 slice prosciutto** (1 ounce), cut in julienne strips
- **4 ounces brown or white mushrooms** (about 4), sliced
- **2 tablespoons dry white wine**
- **1 medium tomato,** peeled, seeded and chopped
- **Salt and pepper**
- **½ teaspoon fresh thyme** (or ¼ teaspoon dried)
- **1 fresh chicken breast half** (5 ounces), skinned and boned

In Italian cooking, pollo alla cacciatora *is "chicken in the hunter's style." Quickly cooked, it most often combines poultry with tomatoes and mushrooms. This recipe adds prosciutto, and as the main course at an Italian dinner table, it might be preceded by a simple first course of* pasta al burro e formaggio*—that is, a good pasta tossed with butter and grated imported Parmesan (Parmigiano-Reggiano).*

With a baking sheet in place, preheat the oven to 400°.

For each serving, lightly spray the center area of a 16" length of foil with olive oil.

In a small skillet, melt the butter. Add the shallot, prosciutto and mushrooms; and sauté for two minutes. Add the wine and stir until it evaporates. Then stir in the tomato and let it cook for 30 seconds. Season with a little salt and pepper, and sprinkle with the thyme.

Make a horizontal slit in the chicken breast, without cutting all the way through. Stuff it with half of the mushroom sauce.

Place the chicken breast on the foil, to one side of its center, and top with the remaining sauce.

Fold the foil over the chicken; then fold and tightly crimp the edges together to form a D-shaped packet. Transfer the packet to the hot baking sheet, and bake for 15 minutes.

On a dinner plate, slit open the packet's straight side and withdraw the foil, leaving the chicken and sauce on the plate.

Note: *Prosciutto is far easier to cut in julienne strips when it's partially frozen.*

Crumbed Chicken Breast

and Roasted Zucchini

Crumbed Chicken Breast

one serving

- **Olive oil spray**
- **1 fresh chicken breast half** (5 ounces), skinned and boned
- **1 ounce Gruyère cheese** (or other Swiss cheese), sliced very thin
- **1 egg** (one will coat two servings)
- **Salt and pepper**
- **½ teaspoon fresh thyme** (or ¼ teaspoon dried)
- **½ cup soft white bread crumbs**

Roasted Zucchini

one serving

- **1 medium zucchini** (5 ounces)
- **Olive oil**
- **Salt and pepper**

Preheat the oven to 400°. Cut the zucchini lengthwise and crossways to make four pieces. Lightly coat them with oil and arrange (skin side up) on a foil-covered baking sheet. Then season with salt and pepper to taste, and bake for 15 minutes.

With the zucchini roasting alongside it in a foil-lined pan, this chicken breast is simple enough to prepare as a dinner for one, yet impressive enough to serve company. The contrast between its crispy coating and melted cheese filling is enticing.

Preheat the oven to 400°.

Line a shallow baking pan with foil, and spray the center area with olive oil.

For each serving, make a horizontal slit in the chicken breast, without cutting all the way through. Fill it with the cheese.

Break the egg into a shallow bowl. Add the thyme, and salt and pepper to taste. Beat well.

Spread the bread crumbs on a plate. Dip the stuffed chicken breast first in the egg and then in the crumbs, pressing them in well. Then transfer it to the baking pan. Lightly spray the chicken with olive oil, and season with salt and pepper to taste.

Bake the chicken about 15 minutes, until the cheese is melted. Serve with the zucchini pieces, browned side up.

Note: *The zucchini can be cooked in the baking pan alongside the chicken breast.*

Chicken Breast in Chard

with Walnut Dressing

Chicken Breast in Chard
one serving

- **2 large chard leaves** (about 4" wide)
- **½ tablespoon butter**
- **1 teaspoon olive oil**
- **1 large shallot,** finely chopped
- **2 tablespoons ham** (or Canadian-style bacon), finely chopped
- **¼ cup coarsely chopped walnuts**
- **½ teaspoon fresh thyme** (or ¼ teaspoon dried)
- **Salt and pepper**
- **Olive oil spray**
- **1 fresh chicken breast half** (5 ounces), skinned and boned

This combination of complementary flavors and different textures turns a simple chicken breast into an elegant entrée for a special dinner.

With a baking sheet in place, preheat the oven to 400°.

Bring a large pot of water to a boil. Rinse the chard leaves. Cut off their stems, chop them finely, and reserve. Drop the leaves into the boiling water to cook for one minute. Remove them with a slotted spoon, and immediately plunge them into cold water to set their color, then drain.

In a skillet, heat the butter and olive oil. Add the chopped chard stems, shallot, ham and walnuts. Season with the thyme and salt and pepper to taste. Over medium heat, stir often until the stems and shallot have softened, about five minutes.

For each serving, lightly spray the center area of a 16" length of foil with olive oil. Lay one chard leaf to one side of its center, and top it with the chicken breast. Season with salt and pepper. Bring the ends of the leaf up around the chicken breast, then wrap the second leaf across and completely around the chicken. (The leaves will cling to each other.) Top with the walnut dressing.

Fold the foil over the chicken; then fold and tightly crimp the edges together to form a D-shaped packet. Transfer the packet to the hot baking sheet, and bake for 15 minutes.

On a dinner plate, slit open the packet's straight side and withdraw the foil, leaving the chard-wrapped chicken and walnuts on the plate.

Note: *If preparing the packets ahead of time, let the dressing cool before adding it to the chicken. (If the packets are made more than 30 minutes ahead, keep them refrigerated and bake them for two minutes longer.) This is a sensible safety measure to prevent any bacteria on the uncooked chicken from multiplying—they like warmth.*

Deviled Chicken Leg
with a Breaded Crust

Deviled Chicken Leg
one serving

- **1 whole chicken leg** (8 ounces)
- **Olive oil spray**
- **3 tablespoons soft white bread crumbs** *(see page 122)*
- **½ tablespoon Dijon mustard** (smooth or whole grain)

The "devil" here is a reference to the hotness of the Dijon mustard coating—a rather minor devil that on a scale of one to ten would rate about a two. The combination of mustard and bread crumbs lends delicious flavor and an appealing crispness, so you get the pleasure of fried chicken with none of the drawbacks.

With a foil-lined baking sheet in place, preheat the oven to 425°.

For each serving, prepare the chicken by chopping off the knobby bone at the end of the drumstick. (This severs the tendons, making the cooked chicken leg far easier to cut.) Then remove and discard the skin and any excess fat.

Spray the flat side of the chicken leg with olive oil, and turn it over. Spread the mustard on the rounded side, and top it with the bread crumbs, pressing them in well. Then spray with olive oil.

Transfer the chicken to the hot baking sheet, crumbed side up, and bake for 25 minutes, until cooked through and crispy on the outside.

Note: *Chicken leg bones are surprisingly supple and easily cut through with a good whack from a chef's knife or cleaver. Do check for any sharp little splinters that may be left in the meat.*

Tarragon Chicken Breast
with Mushroom Sauce

Tarragon Chicken Breast
one serving

- **1½ tablespoons butter,** softened
- **1 large shallot,** finely chopped
- **¼ teaspoon dried tarragon**
- **4 ounces white mushrooms** (about 4), sliced
- **1 tablespoon pale dry Spanish sherry**
- **Salt and pepper**
- **2 tablespoons heavy cream**
- **1 fresh chicken breast half** (5 ounces), skinned and boned

The subtle lemon-licorice taste of tarragon complements the chicken, enhancing without overwhelming its own flavor. Fresh tarragon can be difficult to find; but if you have it, use double the amount of the dried leaves, and garnish the chicken breast with a fresh sprig.

With a baking sheet in place, preheat the oven to 400°.

For each serving, grease the center area of a 16" length of foil with ½ tablespoon of the butter.

In a skillet, melt the remaining butter. Add the shallot, and cook two minutes, until just softened. Stir in the tarragon and mushrooms, and sauté until barely cooked, about three minutes. Stir in the sherry, and season with salt and pepper to taste. Then add the cream, and let it simmer for 30 seconds, stirring frequently.

Transfer half the mushroom sauce to the foil, to one side of its center. Top it with the chicken breast and the remaining sauce.

Fold the foil over the chicken; then fold and tightly crimp the edges together to form a D-shaped packet. Transfer the packet to the hot baking sheet, and bake for 15 minutes.

On a dinner plate, slit open the packet's straight side and withdraw the foil, leaving the chicken and mushroom sauce on the plate.

Note: *I always serve this with plain white rice (page 39), also cooked in the oven. If the packets of chicken and bowl of rice go in at the same time, the rice will be done a few minutes after the chicken. By then, the chicken and mushroom sauce will have been transferred from the packets onto the dinner plates, ready for the rice to be added.*

Roasted Chicken Provençal

with Red Bell Peppers and Black Olives

Roasted Chicken Provençal
four to six servings

- **1 fresh roasting chicken** (5½ to 6 pounds)
- **1 cup black olives,** pitted
- **5 tablespoons butter,** softened
- **1 teaspoon Herbes de Provence**
- **Salt and pepper**
- **4 red bell peppers,** halved and peeled

Pan Sauce
six servings

- **Pan juices,** fat removed
- **¼ cup boiling water**
- **¾ cup chicken broth**
- **Salt and pepper**

This Mediterranean combination is typical of the cooking of southern France: rustic and savory.

Preheat the oven to 375°. Line a roasting pan with heavy-duty foil, and position a roasting rack in it.

Remove the giblets and any excess fat. Rinse the chicken inside and out, and pat it dry with paper towels. Place the olives in the cavity. Fold the third joint of the wings back, and tuck them under the bird. (This will allow heat to penetrate the untrussed meat quickly and evenly.)

Rub the underside with one tablespoon of the butter. Place the chicken on the rack; rub its top and sides with one tablespoon of the butter, and season it with the Herbes de Provence, salt and pepper. Place a heart-shaped piece of foil over the breast *(see Note).* In a small saucepan, melt the remaining butter for basting.

Roast the chicken for 20 minutes per pound (about two hours), basting it every 15 minutes, first with the melted butter and then with the juices in the roasting pan.

About 15 minutes before the chicken is done, remove the foil that covers the breast to allow browning. Then add the bell pepper halves to the pan. (When the chicken is done, a meat thermometer inserted in the thigh should register 160° to 165°.)

Remove the pan from the oven. Using a slotted spoon, transfer the olives from the cavity of the chicken to a warm serving platter. Using a bulb baster, transfer the juices from the cavity to a saucepan.

Note: *Placing a piece of foil over the tender breast meat prevents it from drying out while the legs cook through. Fold a sheet of foil in half and cut it into a half-heart shape, about 7" long and 3" wide. Unfold it, and gently shape it over the breast before the chicken goes into the oven. Removing it before the chicken is done will allow the breast to brown.*

Transfer the chicken and bell pepper halves to the platter, and arrange the peppers and olives around it. Cover the platter with a foil tent to keep the chicken warm while it rests for ten minutes.

Carve the chicken, and serve it with the bell peppers and olives. Pass the sauce separately.

Pan Sauce

Remove and discard the fat from the juices left in the roasting pan. Add the boiling water to the pan, and stir with a wooden spoon to loosen any brown particles, being careful not to tear the foil. Add this mixture to the saucepan of juices taken from the chicken cavity. Stir in the chicken broth, and bring to a simmer. (The sauce will be clear and thin.) Taste and season the sauce with salt and pepper before pouring it into a warm sauceboat.

Note: *Herbes de Provence is the label for a mixture of dried thyme, basil, savory, fennel and lavender sold in specialty food shops. You can easily blend a supply to suit your own taste.*

Lebanese Chicken
with Tahini Sauce

Lebanese Chicken
four servings

- **8 chicken thighs** (2½ pounds total)
- **Sweet paprika**
- **Salt and pepper** (preferably fresh ground)
- **2 garlic cloves,** finely chopped
- **2 tablespoons olive oil**
- **2 tablespoons lemon juice**
- **1 bunch of watercress**
- **1 lemon,** cut in 4 wedges

Tahini Sauce
four servings (1 cup)

- **1 large garlic clove**
- **½ teaspoon salt**
- **⅛ teaspoon cayenne**
- **1 cup tahini paste**
- **Juice of 1 lemon**

The cooking of the Eastern Mediterranean is endlessly seductive, with its brilliant colors and flavors. The perfect first course with this Lebanese dish would be a salad of tomato slices drizzled with olive oil and lemon juice, and garnished with black olives, toasted pine nuts, chopped chives and crumbled feta cheese.

Sprinkle each chicken thigh on both sides with paprika, salt and pepper, rubbing them in well. Place the chicken in a shallow dish.

Mash the garlic cloves with the olive oil, then beat in the lemon juice. Pour this mixture over the chicken, turning the pieces so they're coated all over. Cover and refrigerate for two hours, or overnight if time permits.

Preheat the broiler, and line a broiler pan with foil. Transfer the chicken from the marinade to the broiler pan. Broil 20 to 25 minutes, turning each three or four times, until well browned on the outside but still juicy within. (The juices should run clear when the meat is pierced with the tip of a knife.)

On a platter, arrange the chicken thighs on a bed of watercress. Serve garnished with lemon wedges, and pass the Tahini Sauce separately.

Tahini Sauce

Crush the garlic clove with the salt and cayenne. Then stir in the tahini paste and lemon juice. Beat well with a fork, and taste for seasoning. Serve the sauce in a bowl at room temperature.

Note: *Tahini paste (made from ground, toasted sesame seeds and water) can be found in any Middle Eastern grocery store, many supermarkets and natural-foods stores. Leftover tahini sauce will keep refrigerated for one week (or can be frozen). It makes an excellent dip with raw vegetables.*

Curried Chicken

Served with White Rice

Curried Chicken
one serving

- **2 teaspoons mild vegetable oil**
- **1 small onion,** chopped
- **1 garlic clove,** finely chopped
- **1 small, crisp apple,** peeled, cored and chopped
- **1 tablespoon raisins**
- **1/4 teaspoon cumin**
- **1/4 teaspoon turmeric**
- **1/4 teaspoon coriander**
- **1/4 teaspoon cinnamon**
- **1/4 teaspoon hot red pepper flakes**
- **1 fresh chicken breast half** (5 ounces), skinned and boned, cut in 1" chunks
- **Salt**
- **2 tablespoons tomato puree**
- **1/4 cup plain yogurt**
- **White Rice** *(see page 39)*

Indian curry dishes often have a more subtle, less fiery flavor than you would imagine. That lightness and delicacy characterize this entrée with its tomato yogurt sauce. Serve it with white rice, preferably an aromatic basmati from India.

With a baking sheet in place, preheat the oven to 425°.

In a skillet, heat the oil, and add the onion, garlic, apple and raisins. Sauté until the onion softens, three to four minutes. Sprinkle with the cumin, turmeric, coriander, cinnamon and pepper flakes. Stir for 30 seconds, to bring out their fragrance. Then remove from the heat.

Stir in the chicken, and season to taste with salt.

For each serving, spoon the chicken mixture onto a 16" length of foil, to one side of its center. Fold the foil over it; then fold and tightly crimp the edges together to form a D-shaped packet.

Transfer the packet to the hot baking sheet, and bake for 12 minutes.

Meanwhile, in the same skillet, combine the tomato puree and yogurt, and heat gently (without boiling).

Over the skillet, slit open the packet's straight side, and add the chicken and sauce to the yogurt mixture. Stir gently.

Spoon the mixture onto a dinner plate beside the rice.

Note: *In most cases the flavor of olive oil is a welcome addition to a cooked dish and a healthful substitute for butter. The exception is Asian foods. Olive oil doesn't marry well with Asian spices, so use a mild-flavored vegetable oil instead.*

Roasted Chicken Legs
with Spinach-Almond Stuffing

Roasted Chicken Legs
four servings

- **Olive oil spray**
- **Spinach-Almond Stuffing**
- **4 whole fresh chicken legs** (about 8 ounces each), with skin
- **1 tablespoon butter,** melted
- **Salt and pepper**

Spinach-Almond Stuffing
four servings (1½ cups)

- **1 tablespoon olive oil**
- **2 large shallots** (or 1 small onion), chopped
- **1 garlic clove,** chopped
- **½ cup whole almonds, ground**
- **½ cup thawed, frozen spinach**
- **¼ cup grated imported Parmesan**
- **1 teaspoon fresh chopped oregano** (or ½ teaspoon dried)
- **¼ cup soft white bread crumbs**
- **½ teaspoon salt**
- **¼ teaspoon pepper**
- **1 egg**

A savory, herb-scented stuffing can turn the most ordinary poultry parts into something special. In this case, the chicken legs are stuffed under their skin with a mixture of spinach, imported Parmesan cheese and, for good texture, ground almonds to fill out and flavor the meat.

Preheat the oven to 375°. Line a shallow roasting pan with foil, and lightly spray the foil with olive oil.

Begin by preparing the stuffing *(see recipe below).*

With your fingers, gently loosen the skin of the chicken legs away from the meat, without detaching it at the sides. Insert one fourth of the stuffing under the skin of each chicken leg, shaping it evenly from the outside with your hand.

Brush the chicken legs with the butter, then season them with salt and pepper to taste.

Arrange the chicken legs with the stuffed side up in the pan. Roast for 35 minutes, until brown and tender, basting twice with the pan juices after the first 20 minutes.

Spinach-Almond Stuffing

In a small skillet, heat the olive oil. Add the shallot and garlic, and cook gently until softened but not browned, about three minutes. Transfer to a bowl. Add the almonds, spinach, Parmesan, oregano, bread crumbs, salt, pepper and egg. Mix well.

Note: *When preparing individual chicken legs for cooking, chop off the knobby bone at the end of each drumstick with a chef's knife or cleaver. This makes the meat far easier to cut from the bone when it's served.*

Crispy Chicken Wings
in the Eastern Mediterranean Style

Crispy Chicken Wings
four servings

- **18 chicken wings** (4 pounds total)
- **1/4 cup olive oil**
- **Juice of large lemon half**
- **1 tablespoon chopped fresh oregano**
- **1/2 teaspoon cumin**
- **1/2 teaspoon allspice**
- **1/4 teaspoon chili powder**
- **1/2 teaspoon salt**
- **1/4 teaspoon pepper** (preferably fresh ground)
- **Fresh oregano sprigs**

A gloriously informal dish, this is "finger food" at its finest. And baking the wings on a foil-lined pan saves a lot of tiresome cleanup. (Remember to provide lots of paper napkins!)

Rinse the chicken wings, and pat them dry with a paper towel. Chop off and discard the wing tips; then cut each wing through the joint into two sections.

In a shallow bowl, combine the olive oil, lemon juice, oregano, cumin, allspice, chili powder, salt and pepper. Add the chicken wing pieces, turning to coat each side. Cover the bowl with foil, refrigerate and marinate for one hour.

Preheat the oven to 425°, and line a shallow baking pan with foil.

Remove the wings from the marinade, and arrange them spaced apart on the baking sheet. Bake for 20 minutes, then turn the wings over with tongs, baste them with the marinade, and continue baking about ten minutes, until crispy.

Transfer the wings to a serving platter, and garnish with fresh oregano sprigs. (Allow them to cool slightly before serving, or else they'll be too hot to handle.)

Note: *For a casual buffet dinner, serve the chicken wings with other Mediterranean-style finger foods: bite-size raw vegetables (cherry tomatoes, cucumber and zucchini) accompanied by Tahini Sauce (page 54), bowls of black and green olives, cubed feta cheese and crusty Flat Breads (pages 93 and 94).*

Persian-Style Roast Chicken
with Dried-Fruit Stuffing

Persian-Style Roast Chicken
four servings

- **Olive oil spray**
- **1 fresh roasting chicken** (about 4 pounds)
- **Dried-Fruit Stuffing**
- **1 tablespoon butter,** softened
- **Salt**
- **¼ cup fresh orange juice**
- **1 lime,** cut in 4 wedges, for garnish
- **Chicken broth** (if needed for the pan sauce)

Traditional Persian cuisine transforms readily available ingredients into dishes that are profoundly different, yet very appealing to most Western palates. This roasted chicken stuffed with dried fruits and pistachios is simple to prepare.

Preheat the oven to 350°.

Line a roasting pan with foil and lightly spray it with olive oil.

Remove the giblets and any excess fat. Rinse the chicken inside and out, pat it dry with paper towels, and set it aside.

Begin by preparing the stuffing *(see recipe opposite).* Stuff the cavity of the chicken. Close the openings with poultry pins.

Rub the chicken with the butter, and season it with salt. Place it in the roasting pan, and pour the orange juice over it. Tightly cover the pan with foil, and bake the chicken about one hour and 15 minutes, until very tender.

Then remove the foil and baste the chicken with the syrupy pan juices. With a bulb baster, transfer the remaining juices to a small saucepan for making the pan sauce.

Return the chicken to the oven, and roast it uncovered for ten minutes more, until lightly browned. Then transfer it to a warm platter. Lightly cover the chicken with a foil tent to keep it warm while it rests for ten minutes.

Make the pan sauce. Carve the chicken and serve each portion with one fourth of the the stuffing and a lime wedge for squeezing over the chicken. Pass the sauce separately.

Note: *In most cases a whole chicken is best roasted on an open rack to promote a crispy skin. However, a number of ethnic recipes call for cooking it covered "until the meat is falling off the bones." That's the intent of this recipe, and the succulent meat is utterly delicious this way.*

Dried-Fruit Stuffing
four servings (1¼ cups)

- **2 teaspoons olive oil**
- **½ onion,** chopped
- **1 large garlic clove,** finely chopped
- **½ tart green apple,** peeled, cored and chopped
- **6 soft pitted prunes,** finely chopped
- **6 soft dried apricots,** finely chopped
- **1 tablespoon Zante currants,** steeped in hot water 10 minutes, then drained
- **¼ cup shelled pistachios**
- **Zest of half an orange,** finely shredded
- **Salt and pepper**
- **⅛ teaspoon cinnamon**
- **⅛ teaspoon ground cloves**
- **⅛ teaspoon ground cumin**

Dried-Fruit Stuffing

In a skillet, heat the oil and add the onion and garlic. Cook until soft but not browned, about five minutes.

Add the apple, prunes, apricots, currants, pistachios and orange zest. Season with salt (sparingly if the pistachios are already salted), a generous grinding of pepper, the cinnamon, cloves and cumin. Stir over medium heat for one minute. Remove the stuffing from the heat, and let it cool.

Pan Sauce

Remove and discard the fat from the juices left in the roasting pan. Heat the remaining liquid in a small saucepan, adding a little chicken broth if it's very thick. Taste for seasoning, and serve in a warm sauceboat.

Note: *If you don't happen to have a fat separator for removing the fats from the clear cooking juices, place a container of pan juices in the freezer to cool for ten minutes. By then the fat will have risen to the top and can be easily lifted out and discarded, leaving only the chicken's flavorful juices.*

Roasted Turkey Breast
with Turkey Gravy

Roasted Turkey Breast
four servings

- **1 half-breast of fresh turkey with bone** (3 pounds)
- **3 tablespoons butter,** softened
- **2 tablespoons grated hard cheese** (Parmesan, Dry Jack or pecorino)
- **2 teaspoons all-purpose flour** (or brown rice flour)
- **1 teaspoon fresh thyme,** or ½ teaspoon dried
- **Salt and pepper**
- **2 strips lemon zest,** each 1" x 3"

Turkey Gravy
four servings

- **Pan juices**
- **1 teaspoon cornstarch** (or potato starch), dissolved in 1 tablespoon water or white wine

Steamed in a large foil packet with aromatic thyme and lemon, the moist meat of a mild-tasting turkey breast absorbs their fresh, bright flavors. If you're using fresh thyme, garnish each serving with a sprig or two.

Preheat the oven to 350°.

Smear the center area of a 20" length of heavy-duty foil with one tablespoon of the butter.

Rinse the turkey breast, then pat it dry with paper towels.

In a saucepan over very low heat, slowly melt the remaining butter, and stir in the cheese, flour, thyme, ½ teaspoon salt and a generous grinding of pepper.

Place the turkey breast on the foil, spread the butter mixture over its skin, and tuck the lemon zest underneath the meat. Lift the two long sides of the foil over the turkey breast, double folding them together. Then fold each end twice to form an airtight packet.

Transfer the packet to a shallow baking pan, and bake two hours.

Carefully unfold the foil, transfer the turkey to a warm platter, and reserve the juices for gravy. Slice the meat, and serve with the gravy poured over it.

Turkey Gravy

About ⅔ cup of juices will collect inside the foil packet. Pour them into a small saucepan, bring to a boil and stir in the cornstarch. Let it simmer for a few seconds, stirring until it thickens and clears. Taste for seasoning.

Note: *In the case of poultry that is processed and sold by the separate part, foil-packet cooking has a decided advantage over roasting the meat in an open pan in the dry heat of an oven. And since the meat is less likely to come from a free-range bird, the moist packet compensates by promoting tenderness and flavor without basting.*

Rolled Turkey Roast
with Sausage Stuffing

Rolled Turkey Roast
two servings

- **1 turkey thigh** (1½ pounds), boned, with the skin left on
- **Salt and pepper**
- **2 English-style pork sausages** (4 ounces total)
- **½ cup chopped parsley**
- **1 tablespoon butter,** softened

Preparation
To bone the turkey thigh: Place the meat skin-side down on a work surface. Using a short, very sharp knife, cut and scrape along and around the bone and knobby joint until the bone can be lifted free, leaving the meat still attached to the skin. Be sure to cut away any bits of tough cartilage still embedded in the meat.

Mildly seasoned English-style pork sausages, fondly known as "bangers," are good for stuffing a boneless turkey roast. Since the sausages contain bread crumbs, they expand rather than shrink while cooking, which is an asset in a stuffing. In case you're wondering, they're called "bangers" because if pan-fried too quickly, they sizzle with a popping sound, and the thin casings are inclined to burst open.

Preheat the oven to 350°, and line a roasting pan with foil.

Bone the turkey thigh *(see Preparation).* Place the turkey, skin-side down, on a work surface. Trim the meat to a rectangle about 6" by 8" that can be rolled evenly. (The trimmings can be frozen for later use in a soup or stir-fry dish.) Season with salt and pepper.

Slit and remove the casings from the sausages. Then press the sausage meat together, and roll it in the chopped parsley, elongating to form a 7" loaf. Place it on top of the turkey; then roll the turkey to enclose the filling, and tie the roll at 1" intervals with butcher's twine to make a long sausage shape.

Place the rolled turkey with its seam-side down in the pan, and rub it with the butter.

Roast the turkey about 45 minutes, basting several times with the pan juices. (A meat thermometer should register 170°.)

Transfer the turkey to a warm platter, cover loosely with a foil tent, and let it rest for ten minutes. Slice the turkey roll, removing the twine. Arrange the slices on dinner plates.

Note: *If you cannot find English bangers, substitute four ounces of pork sausage meat mixed with ¼ cup of white bread crumbs, a pinch of dried sage and a pinch of ground nutmeg.*

Classic Holiday Turkey
with Brown Rice and Sausage Stuffing

Classic Holiday Turkey
eight servings

- **1 fresh turkey** (12 pounds)
- **1 lemon,** cut in half
- **1 bunch parsley,** rinsed and dried
- **½ cup butter,** softened
- **Salt and pepper**
- **1 cup water**

Turkey Roasting Times and Servings (*for a 325° oven*)		
Weight	**Time**	**Servings**
8 lb.	2½ hours	6
12 lb.	3 hours	8
16 lb.	3¾ hours	10
20 lb.	4½ hours	12–14

For the best flavor and texture, insist on a fresh, organically raised turkey weighing 1½ pounds per person. This ensures generous servings with leftovers, which some of us rightly consider to be the highlight of this whole exercise! This recipe is for a 12-pound bird; check the chart below for other weights and their cooking times. Because turkeys vary in shape according to their breed, cooking times are approximate. A meat thermometer inserted in the thickest part of the thigh (without touching the bone) will ensure that the meat inside is perfectly done.

Classic Holiday Turkey

Preheat the oven to 325°.

Remove the neck and giblets from the cavity; rinse the turkey inside and out, and pat it dry with paper towels. Tuck the legs under the skin band; fold the third joint of the wings back, and tuck them under the bird.

Place the lemon halves and the parsley inside the cavity. Rub the turkey all over with the butter, and season with salt and pepper.

Place it breast-side up on a rack in a roasting pan, and pour the water into the pan. Cover the breast with foil *(see Note),* leaving the wings and thighs exposed.

Roast for two hours, basting with pan juices every 20 minutes. Then remove the foil cover.

Continue roasting 30 to 45 minutes more, until the meat thermometer registers 175° to 180°.

Transfer the bird to a warm platter, and cover it loosely with a foil tent. Let it rest for 20 minutes before carving.

Note: *Placing a piece of foil over the tender breast meat prevents it from drying out while the legs cook through. Fold a sheet of foil in half, and cut it into a half-heart shape, about 16" long and 8" wide. Unfold and gently shape it over the breast before the turkey goes into the oven. Removing the foil before the turkey is done will allow the breast to brown.*

Brown Rice and Sausage Stuffing

eight servings (8 to 10 cups)

- **1 cup brown rice** (medium- or long-grain)
- **Olive oil spray**
- **1½ teaspoons fennel seeds**
- **2 cups boiling chicken broth**
- **4 tablespoons butter**
- **3 sweet Italian sausages** (12 ounces total), casings removed
- **1½ cups chopped onion**
- **2 cups finely chopped celery**
- **½ cup chopped walnuts,** lightly toasted in a dry skillet
- **Salt and pepper**

Preheat the oven to 350°. Line a shallow baking pan with foil, and spread the rice on it. Bake for eight minutes, until the grains puff.

Lightly spray the interior of a two-quart (eight-cup) oven-safe bowl with olive oil, and transfer the rice to it. Add the fennel seeds, boiling broth and one tablespoon of the butter. Tightly cover the bowl with foil, and bake for 45 minutes. Carefully remove the foil. Fluff the rice with a fork, and let it rest for ten minutes, loosely covered with foil. (Reduce the oven temperature to 325°.)

In a skillet over medium heat, crumble the sausage and cook until it is no longer pink, about five minutes, breaking up any lumps. Pour off the fat, and transfer the sausage to a food processor. Process until finely ground.

In the same skillet, heat the remaining butter. Add the onion, and cook over low heat, stirring occasionally, until soft, eight to ten minutes. Stir in the celery, and cook until tender-crisp, five minutes.

In a large bowl, combine the sausage, celery mixture, rice and walnuts. Season with salt and pepper to taste. Spoon the stuffing into a buttered, two-quart (eight-cup) baking dish. Tightly cover it with foil, and bake at 325° for 30 minutes.

Turkey Gravy

eight servings (2 cups)

- **4 tablespoons pan juices**
- **3 tablespoons all-purpose flour** (or brown rice flour)
- **Salt and pepper**
- **2 cups chicken broth**

Discard most of the fat from the roasting pan, and transfer the remaining pan juices (with their brown particles) into a saucepan. Over medium heat, add the flour, and stir until lightly browned, about three minutes. Season with salt and pepper. Gradually pour in the broth, stirring until smooth. Simmer gently for ten minutes, and taste for seasoning before transferring to a sauceboat.

Note: *It's always easier (and safer) to assemble the stuffing in advance and bake it separately. This fennel-scented, savory stuffing may be made one day ahead. Allow it to cool after combining the cooked ingredients, then cover and refrigerate. Bring it to room temperature before baking.*

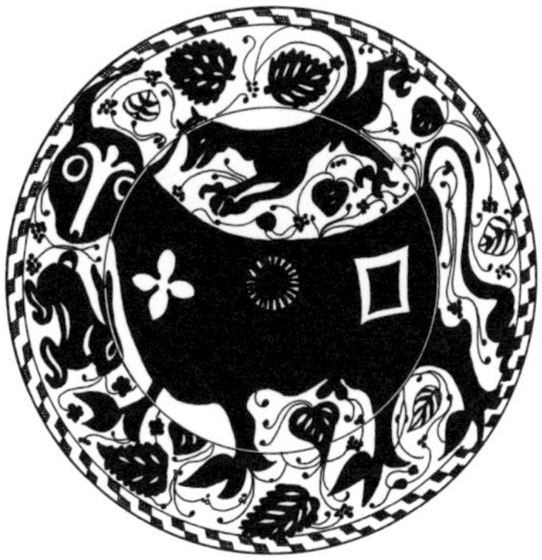

Meats

THE EXPRESSION "do the honors" comes to us from the ceremonial carving of roasted meats at Medieval banquet tables, where the relative size of a portion and the order in which it was served designated the diner's rank at the table. Meat is still the centerpiece of many a traditional dinner, but in doing the honors these days, we serve it more evenhandedly.

Beef, lamb and pork—the hearty meats most favored as a main course—present a challenge to foil-packet cookery. While quick steaming tends to toughen their fibers and dull their taste, slow cooking is another matter. Gently braising lean pieces of lamb in a packet with slices of potato and onion for moisture and flavor results in a meltingly tender stew. And a slice of smoked ham cooked in a packet with peas and cream is absolutely delicious.

Roasting (rather than panfrying) small cuts of meat benefits from the use of a preheated, foil-lined baking pan. The hot foil quickly sears the meat on the outside, while the inside roasts to succulent perfection. Later, the foil liner makes cleanup that much easier. For a crown roast with a rice and eggplant stuffing, lining the pan with heavy-duty foil makes no difference in the way the lamb cooks, but it serves me well as a sort of sling for transferring the finished roast with its stuffing intact to a platter.

Savory Meat Patties
of Beef and Veal

Savory Meat Patties
two servings

- **½ pound ground beef chuck**
- **¼ pound ground veal**
- **1 egg yolk**
- **½ cup soft white bread crumbs** *(see page 122)*
- **½ teaspoon grated lemon zest**
- **¼ teaspoon ground nutmeg**
- **½ teaspoon fresh thyme** (or ¼ teaspoon dried)
- **½ teaspoon salt**
- **¼ teaspoon pepper**
- **Olive oil spray**

These are European-style meat patties as opposed to familiar American hamburgers. With their smoother texture, they're more like savory little meat loaves. The ground veal is slightly gelatinous, which helps to hold the ingredients together. They freeze well, individually wrapped, so it's worth doubling the recipe (in which case you'll use a whole egg rather than two yolks). Serve them with the Oven-Fried Potato Wedges on page 31 and the Mushroom Sauce on page 68 (or your own tomato sauce).

With a foil-lined shallow baking pan in place, preheat the oven to 425°.

In a large bowl, combine the beef, veal, egg yolk, bread crumbs, lemon zest, nutmeg, thyme, salt and pepper. Mix the ingredients by hand or with a wooden spoon to form a smooth paste.

Divide and shape the meat mixture into two oval patties, about 1" thick. Spray both sides of each with olive oil.

Transfer the patties to the hot pan, and roast for seven minutes. Turn them over, spray again with olive oil, and roast seven minutes more for medium-rare, or longer for well-done.

Remove the pan from the oven, and loosely cover the patties with a foil tent, letting them rest for five minutes. Then transfer them to warm dinner plates.

Note: *Having the meats ground to order by a butcher is recommended.*

Filet Mignon
with Mushroom Sauce

Filet Mignon
one serving

- **1 filet mignon** (5 ounces, 1" thick)
- **Pepper**
- **2 slices pancetta** (1/2 ounce each)
- **Olive oil**

Mushroom Sauce
two servings (one cup)

- **1/2 ounce dried porcini mushrooms**
- **1 tablespoon olive oil**
- **2 large garlic cloves,** thinly sliced
- **1 large shallot,** finely chopped
- **1 ounce pancetta,** finely chopped
- **4 ounces small brown mushrooms** (about 4), sliced
- **1/2 teaspoon fresh thyme** (or 1/4 teaspoon dried)
- **Salt and pepper**
- **1 tablespoon brandy**
- **1/2 teaspoon cornstarch,** dissolved in 1 tablespoon cold water

A thick filet mignon can be roasted to medium-rare perfection if sandwiched between layers of pancetta, that spicy Italian bacon.

Filet Mignon

With a foil-lined shallow baking pan in place, preheat the oven to 425°. Season the filet with pepper, and press a slice of pancetta onto both sides. Spray the pancetta with olive oil.

Transfer the filet to the hot pan, and roast for five minutes. Then turn it over and roast another five minutes for medium-rare, or a little longer for well-done.

Remove the pan from the oven, and loosely cover the filet with a foil tent. Let it rest for five minutes, allowing the juices to settle.

Transfer the filet to a warm dinner plate, and spoon half of the mushroom sauce onto the plate before serving.

Mushroom Sauce

Soak the porcini in 1/2 cup of hot water for 20 minutes. Reserve the liquid, and finely chop the mushrooms. In a skillet, heat the oil; add the garlic, shallot and pancetta; and sauté until the shallot is soft but not browned, about five minutes. Add the porcini, the brown mushrooms and thyme. Season with salt and pepper, and sauté until the mushrooms have softened, about five minutes. Add the brandy, and let it evaporate; then stir in the reserved liquid, and simmer for three minutes. Add the cornstarch, and stir until the sauce thickens and clears, about 30 seconds. Add more water if the sauce is too thick.

Note: *Cured in salt and spices, pancetta is available at Italian delis, where it's sliced from what appears to be a long, fat sausage. For most recipes, prosciutto or thinly cut Canadian-style bacon can substitute for it. The mushroom sauce (which stands on its own as a side dish) can be made ahead and reheated, but thicken it with the cornstarch only just before serving.*

Lamb Stew

with Potato and Onion

Lamb Stew
one serving

- **Olive oil spray**
- **1 medium-large russet potato** (6 to 8 ounces), peeled and sliced ½" thick
- **½ medium onion,** sliced
- **4 ounces lean lamb stew meat** (boneless), cut in ¾" cubes
- **½ teaspoon fresh thyme** (or rosemary), or ¼ teaspoon dried
- **Salt and pepper**
- **4 ice cubes**
- **Chopped parsley**

Jim Beard once described one particular lamb stew he'd enjoyed as "so wonderful you could cuddle it in your arms." A rustic, savory stew is a meal unto itself, and a supremely comforting one at that. Foil-packet cooking allows you to prepare stews in small amounts in a relatively short time, and it's the only way I know to accomplish this feat with success.

With a baking sheet in place, preheat the oven to 350°.

For each serving, lightly spray the center area of a 16" length of foil with olive oil. Arrange the potato slices to one side of its center, and top them with the onion and lamb. Add the thyme, salt and pepper to taste, and the ice cubes.

Fold the foil over the ingredients; then fold and tightly crimp the edges together to form a D-shaped packet. Transfer the packet to the hot baking sheet, and bake for 1½ hours.

On a dinner plate, slit open the packet's straight side and withdraw the foil, leaving the stew on the plate. Sprinkle with the chopped parsley before serving.

Note: *The potato slices will absorb the juices of the lamb and onion, and begin to fall apart. This is supposed to happen.*

Crown Roast of Lamb
with Rice and Eggplant Stuffing

Crown Roast of Lamb
eight servings

- **1 crown roast of lamb** (16 chops), all fat removed
- **Rice and Eggplant Stuffing**
- **Lemon wedges**
- **Fresh sprigs of mint**

Preparation
Have your butcher prepare a crown roast from two 8-rib racks of lamb. Specify that he crack the chine bone between each rib to facilitate carving, remove the fell and all the fat, "French" the bones *(see Note),* and stitch the racks together. He should save all the lean meat trimmings and grind them for the stuffing, adding enough extra lamb meat to make one pound.

You may have to be insistent about his removing *all* the fat from the lamb racks, but you really don't want it to melt into your good stuffing (only to reappear later around your middle).

In the Greek style, this is a spectacular roast for a special occasion. It consists of two rib sections bent and tied in a circle to resemble a crown. Have your butcher prepare it as described in the preparation note below (he'll probably welcome the opportunity to demonstrate this special skill). Not all the delicious eggplant, lamb and rice stuffing will fit inside the crown, so the remainder is baked and served separately.

Crown Roast of Lamb

Preheat the oven to 350°. Line a shallow baking pan with heavy-duty foil, and place the lamb crown in it. Fill the center of the roast with the stuffing.

Spoon the remainder of the stuffing into a baking dish, and set it aside.

Wrap the tips of the bones with foil. Roast for 15 minutes.

Transfer the dish of extra stuffing to the oven with the meat. Continue roasting the meat for 30 minutes for medium-rare, or a little longer for well-done.

Protecting your hands with oven mitts and using the foil as a sling (to keep the stuffing from falling out), transfer the roast to a warm platter. Carefully slip the foil from underneath the meat, and discard the foil covers on the tips of the bones. Garnish the platter with lemon wedges and sprigs of mint.

To carve and serve the roast, cut between the bones to separate the chops, and transfer to dinner plates with some of the stuffing. (The stuffing from the oven can be passed separately at the table.)

Note: *To "French" the bones, cut away all the gristle, thin meat and skin at the top of each rib, leaving them as clean and shiny as possible.*

Rice and Eggplant Stuffing

Start by cooking the rice for the stuffing *(see page 39)*. Let it cool before adding it to the other ingredients.

In a large skillet, heat half the oil. Add the eggplant, and sauté until golden and tender, about ten minutes. Remove and reserve.

In the same skillet, heat the remaining olive oil. Add the onion and celery, and sauté until softened, about five minutes.

Then add the ground lamb, and stir until browned, about seven minutes. Add the parsley, cinnamon, currants, olives, pine nuts and mint. Stir in the reserved rice and the eggplant. Season with salt and pepper.

Rice and Eggplant Stuffing
eight servings

- **1½ cups cooked white rice,** cooled
- **4 tablespoons olive oil**
- **1 small eggplant** (¾ pound), peeled and cut in 1" cubes
- **1 yellow onion,** finely chopped
- **1 celery stalk,** finely chopped
- **1 pound ground lean lamb**
- **½ cup minced parsley**
- **½ teaspoon cinnamon**
- **¼ cup Zante currants**
- **16 ripe kalamata olives,** pitted and chopped
- **½ cup pine nuts**
- **2 tablespoons chopped mint leaves**
- **Salt and pepper**

Note: *Be sure to wrap the tip of each rib with foil before the crown roast goes into the oven; otherwise they'll come out scorched. And for an even more elegant presentation, cover the ends of the cooked ribs with paper frills, which are available from specialty cookware stores.*

Roasted Lamb Rib Chops

with Garlic-Flavored White Beans

Roasted Lamb Rib Chops
two servings

- **2 double rib lamb chops** (7 ounces each, 2" thick)
- **1 teaspoon chopped fresh rosemary** (or 1/4 teaspoon dried)
- **Pepper** (preferably fresh ground)
- **2 thin slices prosciutto** (2 ounces total)
- **Olive oil spray**
- **2 sprigs of fresh rosemary**

Garlic-Flavored White Beans
two servings

- **2 garlic cloves,** finely chopped
- **1/2 onion,** finely chopped
- **1 tablespoon olive oil**
- **One 15-oz. can white beans** (cannellini)
- **1 ripe tomato,** peeled and chopped
- **2 tablespoons chopped parsley**
- **Salt and pepper**

Wrapping thick lamb chops in prosciutto will protect the meat from overcooking and add delicious flavor. Flavored with garlic and tomato, white beans make the perfect accompaniment.

Roasted Lamb Rib Chops

With a foil-lined shallow baking pan in place, preheat the oven to 400°.

Cut all the fat from the lamb chops, including any between the two rib bones, leaving just a nugget of meat attached to the bare bones. Sprinkle with the rosemary and pepper to taste. Wrap a slice of prosciutto around each chop (it will adhere to itself), and lightly spray with olive oil. Transfer the wrapped chops to the hot pan, and roast for 15 minutes for medium-rare, or longer for well-done.

Remove the baking pan from the oven, and loosely cover the chops with a foil tent. Let them rest ten minutes, allowing the juices to settle. (Reserve any pan juices to add to the beans.)

Transfer the chops to warm plates, garnish with sprigs of rosemary, and serve with the beans spooned alongside the chops.

Garlic-Flavored White Beans

In a skillet, sauté the garlic and onion in olive oil until soft but not browned, about five minutes. Add the beans with their liquid, the tomato and parsley. Season with salt and pepper to taste. Simmer for ten minutes. Using the roasting pan's foil liner as a funnel, add any pan juices from the lamb chops to the beans.

Note: *The chops may be prepared several hours ahead of time and kept refrigerated, but be sure to bring them to room temperature before cooking.*

Ham Steak
with Fresh Green Peas

Ham Steak
one serving

- **1 tablespoon butter**
- **1 large shallot,** finely chopped
- **1 slice mild smoked ham** (5 ounces, ½" thick)
- **2 tablespoons heavy cream**
- **¼ cup young green peas,** freshly shelled
- **Pepper**

Frozen peas are so convenient to use that most of us have forgotten what fresh ones taste like. Try shelling some young English peas for a change. Whenever they're available, it can be a revelation.

With a baking sheet in place, preheat the oven to 400°.

In a small skillet, melt the butter. Add the shallot, and cook gently for one minute.

For each serving, spread the cooked shallot over the center area of a 16" length of foil. Place the ham on the foil, to one side of its center, and top with the cream and peas. Season lightly with pepper. Fold the foil over the ham; then fold and tightly crimp the edges together to form a D-shaped packet.

Transfer the packet to the hot baking sheet, and bake for eight minutes.

On a dinner plate, slit open the packet's straight side and withdraw the foil, leaving the ham, peas and sauce on the plate.

Note: *As a flavorful alternative, omit the peas, and smear the ham steak with Dijon mustard.*

Roasted Pork Loin

with Pine Nuts and Garlic

Roasted Pork Loin
four servings

- **1 boneless pork loin** (3 pounds, rolled and tied)
- **25 pine nuts**
- **2 garlic cloves,** cut into slivers
- **1 tablespoon butter,** softened
- **Salt and pepper**
- **½ cup dry white wine**
- **½ cup chicken broth**
- **1 teaspoon cornstarch** (or potato starch), dissolved in 2 tablespoons cold water

Serve this succulent pork roast with Buttered Radishes (page 32). They can go into the already hot oven (with its temperature increased) while the meat is resting and firming up.

Preheat the oven to 350°. Line a roasting pan with foil.

With the pork loin still rolled and tied, place it, fat-side up, on a work surface. Make rows of tiny slits at half-inch intervals over the surface, inserting a pine nut or garlic sliver in each.

Place the meat (fat-side up) in the pan, smear it with the butter, and season with salt and pepper.

Roast for 1¼ to 1½ hours (or 30 minutes per pound), basting occasionally after the first 45 minutes, until a meat thermometer registers 150° and the slightly pink meat is still juicy.

Remove the meat from the oven, and baste once more with the pan juices. Then transfer it to a warm platter, loosely cover it with a foil tent, and let it rest for 10 to 15 minutes.

Meanwhile, remove any excess fat from the pan juices, and add the wine and broth. Stir carefully with a wooden spoon to incorporate any browned bits, and pour into a saucepan. Bring to a boil, and let bubble for five minutes to reduce slightly. Stir in the cornstarch mixture. Let the sauce boil until it thickens and clears, 30 seconds or less. Taste for seasoning.

Carve the meat into ½" thick slices, removing the twine piece by piece as it's carved. Arrange the slices on dinner plates, and spoon the pan sauce on top of each.

Note: *When pork is overcooked, it becomes dry and flavorless. (Old beliefs die hard, but the National Pork Producers Council confirms that pork is perfectly safe to eat after its internal temperature reaches 137°.) Cooking it to 150° gives delicious results.*

Roasted Pork Tenderloin
with Figs and Prosciutto

Roasted Pork Tenderloin
four servings

- **1 pork tenderloin** (12 ounces), trimmed
- **4 thin slices prosciutto** (4 ounces total)
- **6 ripe black figs,** stemmed
- **Olive oil spray**
- **2 small branches fresh sage leaves**
- **½ cup dry white wine**
- **¾ cup chicken broth**
- **Zest of ¼ lemon,** very finely slivered
- **1 teaspoon honey**
- **Salt and pepper**
- **1 teaspoon cornstarch** (or potato starch), dissolved in 2 tablespoons cold water

Some meats and poultry go especially well with certain fruits: Think of pork with apples and duck with oranges. Pork is also delicious with fresh figs, a combination that goes back to Rome in the time of the Caesars.

Preheat the oven to 400°. Line a roasting pan with foil.

Slice the tenderloin lengthwise without cutting all the way through it. Cover with plastic wrap, and pound until it doubles in width.

Arrange three of the prosciutto slices on the meat, and align the figs close together down the center. Starting at one end, roll the meat, prosciutto and figs into a long sausage shape. Top it with the remaining slice of prosciutto, and securely tie it at 1" intervals with butcher's twine. Then lightly spray it all over with olive oil.

Transfer the meat to the roasting pan, tuck the sage underneath the meat, and pour in the wine.

Roast 25 minutes, until just tender. Transfer the meat to a warm platter, loosely cover it with a foil tent, and let it rest for ten minutes.

Discard the sage, and stir to loosen any browned particles. Pour the pan juices into a saucepan. Add the broth, lemon zest and honey; and boil until reduced by one fourth. Season with salt and pepper to taste. Add the cornstarch mixture, and let the sauce bubble until it thickens and clears, about 30 seconds.

Snip off the twine, and slice the tenderloin on the diagonal. Arrange the slices on dinner plates, and spoon the pan sauce on top of each.

Note: *To trim a pork tenderloin for roasting, cut off any silvery skin and the thin tip (which can be frozen for other uses). When fresh figs are not available, substitute soft pitted prunes, simmered in white wine for ten minutes and drained.*

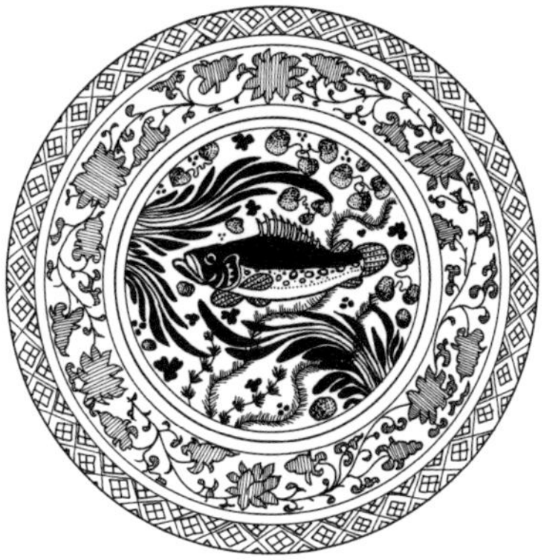

Seafood

FISH STEAMED *en papillote* was a specialty of the master chefs who first cooked with parchment. The results are the same with foil: Fish and scallops come out juicy, flavorful and well textured.

They also cook quickly (most often in ten minutes) in the steam created by their own natural juices. And because the foil packet is airtight, all the nutrients remain intact, with aromas contained until the packet is opened. Anything else added to the packet—wine, mushrooms, herbs and so on—contributes yet more flavor.

Scallops cooked in a skillet too easily become rubbery; but when steamed with sherry, mushrooms and heavy cream in a foil packet, the result is a delicious first course or entrée.

Foil packets of fish can be prepared ahead of time and kept refrigerated for up to three hours. Before baking, allow them to return to room temperature, or add two minutes to the cooking time.

If you can't get absolutely fresh seafood—and it isn't all that easy unless you happen to live near a fishing port—insist upon fish and scallops that have been "individually quick frozen" immediately after they're caught and processed, and not thawed until you're ready to use them.

Fresh Ahi Tuna Salad
with Rosemary Mayonnaise

Fresh Ahi Tuna Salad
two servings

- **Olive oil spray**
- **1 ahi tuna steak** (8 ounces)
- **Salt and pepper**
- **4 branches fresh rosemary** (or 1/2 teaspoon dried)
- **1 tablespoon olive oil**
- **1 cup Rosemary Mayonnaise**
- **Salad greens**

Rosemary Mayonnaise
one cup

- **1 cup mayonnaise**
- **1/8 teaspoon cayenne**
- **1 teaspoon dry mustard powder**
- **2 tablespoons balsamic vinegar**
- **2 teaspoons lemon juice**
- **1/4 teaspoon salt**
- **1/2 teaspoon minced fresh rosemary** (or 1/4 teaspoon dried)

A salad of freshly cooked tuna is totally different from the more familiar sort made from tuna canned in oil—and the difference will amaze you. Flavorful, dark red ahi tuna is becoming increasingly available both fresh and frozen, and it cooks to perfection in a foil packet. A mayonnaise enhanced with rosemary, lemon juice and balsamic vinegar gives this tuna salad its piquant flavor.

Fresh Ahi Tuna Salad

With a baking sheet in place, preheat the oven to 350°.

Spray the center area of a 16" length of foil with olive oil. Place the tuna to one side of its center. Season with salt and pepper, and top with the rosemary.

Fold the foil over the fish; then fold and tightly crimp the edges together to form a D-shaped packet. Transfer the packet to the hot baking sheet, and bake for ten minutes.

Snip open the top of the packet, and drizzle the olive oil over the fish. Let it cool. (If you use rosemary branches, remove and discard them.)

With your fingers or a fork, lightly flake the tuna into a bowl. Then add the Rosemary Mayonnaise, and stir gently to mix.

Divide the greens between two plates, and top with the tuna.

Rosemary Mayonnaise

Place the mayonnaise in a bowl. Add the cayenne, mustard powder, balsamic vinegar, lemon juice, salt and rosemary. Stir well to blend.

Note: *If using dried rosemary instead of fresh, use a mortar and pestle to pulverize any sharp needles.*

Bay Scallops with Roasted Bell Pepper

Served with Spicy Golden Rice

Bay Scallops with Roasted Bell Pepper
one serving

- **Olive oil spray**
- **½ yellow bell pepper,** broiled, peeled and sliced in ¾" diamonds *(see Techniques, page 22)*
- **1 green onion** (including the pale green leaves), chopped
- **1 small ripe tomato,** peeled, seeded and chopped
- **1 teaspoon capers,** drained
- **5 ounces bay scallops**
- **Salt and pepper**
- **1 tablespoon chopped parsley**
- **Spicy Golden Rice** *(see page 39)*

Tiny, sweet bay scallops are at their best when quickly steamed in foil with fresh, aromatic vegetables. (Because of their small size, bay scallops are easily overcooked when they're sautéed on the stovetop.)

Preheat the oven to 400°.

For each serving, lightly spray the center area of a 16" length of foil with olive oil.

Combine the bell pepper, onion, tomato and capers to one side of the center of the foil. Top with the scallops, season with salt and pepper to taste, and sprinkle with the parsley. Spray with olive oil.

Fold the foil over the scallops and vegetables; then fold and tightly crimp the edges together to form a D-shaped packet. Place the packet on a baking sheet, and bake for eight minutes.

On a dinner plate, slit open the packet's straight side and withdraw the foil, leaving the scallop mixture and its aromatic juices on the center of the plate. Spoon the Spicy Golden Rice around the scallops and over their juices.

Note: *If you can't find good fresh scallops, the flash-frozen ones are a fine substitute. As an alternative to tiny bay scallops, cut the larger sea scallops into quarters.*

Bay Scallops with Mushrooms

A First Course or Main Course

Bay Scallops with Mushrooms
one or two servings

- **2 tablespoons butter**
- **1 large shallot,** finely chopped
- **5 ounces small white mushrooms** (about 5), sliced
- **1 tablespoon pale dry Spanish sherry**
- **Salt and white pepper**
- **2 tablespoons heavy cream**
- **5 ounces bay scallops**
- **1/4 cup soft white bread crumbs** *(see page 122)*

This delicate dish bakes quickly in a foil packet—and the recipe is wonderfully versatile. Serve it in shallow soup plates (or natural scallop shells) as an elegant first course for two. Or ladle it over Basil-Flavored Rice (page 39) as a satisfying entrée for one.

Preheat the oven to 400°.

In a nonstick skillet over medium heat, melt half the butter. Add the chopped shallot, and let it simmer for 30 seconds. Stir in the mushrooms, and sauté until softened, about three minutes. Then add the sherry; season with salt and pepper; and stir in the cream. Continue stirring for two minutes. Remove the skillet from the heat, and stir in the scallops.

Prepare a 16" length of foil by turning the sides up slightly to prevent the sauce from escaping. Spoon the scallop mixture to one side of its center. Fold the foil over the scallops; then fold and tightly crimp the edges together to form a D-shaped packet. Place the packet on a baking sheet, and bake for eight minutes.

Meanwhile, wipe the skillet clean with a paper towel. Heat the remaining butter in it. Add the bread crumbs, and stir over medium heat until golden brown and crispy, two minutes or less.

Over a soup plate (or Basil-Flavored Rice on a dinner plate), slit open the packet's straight side and withdraw the foil, leaving the scallops and their sauce on the plate. Sprinkle the crumbs on top before serving.

Note: *Always keep mushrooms refrigerated in a paper bag until they're used. (When stored in plastic, they develop soft spots.) Mushrooms readily absorb moisture, so they should never be soaked in water. A wipe with a damp paper towel is sufficient to clean them before cooking.*

Sea Bass

Stuffed with Fontina Cheese

Sea Bass
one serving

- ½ **tablespoon butter,** softened
- **1 sea bass fillet** (6 ounces)
- **1½ ounces fontina cheese** (or Gruyère), thinly sliced
- **Salt and pepper**
- **1 tablespoon chopped chives** (or green onion, including pale green leaves)

Creamy, golden fontina melted within the sea bass creates a delicious counterpoint to this succulent white fish. Serve it with Oven-Steamed Red Potatoes (page 86) or garlic bread to soak up the fish's savory juices.

With a baking sheet in place, preheat the oven to 425°.

For each serving, smear the center area of a 16" length of foil with the butter.

Place the sea bass on the foil, to one side of its center.

Make a horizontal slit in the fillet (without cutting all the way through it), and insert a double layer of cheese. Then season the fish with salt and pepper, and cover it with the remaining slices of cheese. Sprinkle the chives on top.

Fold the foil over the fish; then fold and tightly crimp the edges together to form a D-shaped packet. Transfer the packet to the hot baking sheet, and bake for ten minutes.

On a dinner plate, slit open the packet's straight side and withdraw the foil, leaving the fish and its juices on the plate.

Note: *Fontina is a firm Italian cheese, a specialty of the Piedmont region. Its flavor is mild and nutty.*

Sea Bass
with Buttered Leeks

Sea Bass
one serving

- **2 tablespoons butter**
- **1 small leek** (white and pale green parts), washed and sliced in 1/4" rings
- **Salt and pepper**
- **1 sea bass fillet** (6 ounces)
- **Pinch of fennel seeds** (or anise seeds)

The leek, a member of the onion family that is too often overlooked, adds its sweet, fresh flavor and crisp green color to this sea bass entrée. If white sea bass is unavailable, use another firm-fleshed white fish such as grouper or striped bass.

With a baking sheet in place, preheat the oven to 425°.

In a skillet, melt the butter. Add the leeks, and cook over low heat until softened but not browned, about eight minutes. Season with salt and pepper to taste.

For each serving, set out a 16" length of foil. Spoon half the leeks to one side of its center, and top with the sea bass. Season it with salt and pepper, and a sprinkling of the fennel seeds. Top with the remaining leeks.

Fold the foil over the fish; then fold and tightly crimp the edges together to form a D-shaped packet. Transfer the packet to the hot baking sheet, and bake for ten minutes.

On a dinner plate, slit open the packet's straight side and withdraw the foil, leaving the fish and leeks on the plate.

Note: *Leeks tend to harbor sand within their beautifully furled leaves, so it's essential to thoroughly wash them. First, cut off the root and tough green leaves, discarding any discolored outer ones. Thinly slice what remains, slosh the slices around in a large bowl of water, and remove the leek. Repeat with fresh water until no sand remains in the bottom of the bowl.*

Halibut with Orange Zest

Served with Almond Rice

Halibut with Orange Zest
one serving

- **½ tablespoon butter,** softened
- **1 halibut steak** (6 ounces)
- **Salt and pepper**
- **Zest of ½ orange,** finely julienned
- **1 teaspoon dry Spanish sherry**
- **⅛ teaspoon ground nutmeg** (preferably freshly grated)
- **Almond Rice** *(See page 39)*

Things that grow together usually go together. This Andalusian combination of orange zest and Spanish sherry lends a special distinction to the halibut's own mild flavor. I serve it with Almond Rice to soak up the aromatic juices of the fish.

With a baking sheet in place, preheat the oven to 425°.

For each serving, smear the center area of a 16" length of foil with the butter.

Place the halibut on the foil, to one side of its center. Season with salt and pepper; top with the orange zest, sherry and nutmeg.

Fold the foil over the fish; then fold and tightly crimp the edges together to form a D-shaped packet. Transfer the packet to the hot baking sheet, and bake for ten minutes.

On a dinner plate, slit open the packet's straight side and withdraw the foil, leaving the fish and its juices on the plate. Spoon the rice around the fish.

Note: *Before zesting the orange, scrub it well under cold water to get rid of any wax or agricultural sprays. Then zest it directly over the fish; the cutting action releases a spray of aromatic citrus oils that shouldn't be wasted.*

Sesame Salmon
with Oven-Steamed Snow Peas

Sesame Salmon
one serving

- **1 teaspoon Asian sesame oil**
- **1 salmon fillet** (5 ounces)
- **1 teaspoon soy sauce**
- **1 teaspoon minced fresh gingerroot**
- **1 garlic clove,** finely chopped
- **½ teaspoon sesame seeds,** lightly toasted in a dry skillet

Oven-Steamed Snow Peas
one serving

- **¼ pound snow peas,** with strings removed
- **Salt**
- **¼ cup water,** boiling

Salmon develops a new personality when teamed with Asian seasonings, but unlike so many of the dishes that originated in the Far East, this one calls for few ingredients and requires little preparation. The snow peas steam in a foil-covered baking dish while the fish cooks in its foil packet.

Sesame Salmon

With a baking sheet in place, preheat the oven to 425°.

For each serving, smear the center area of a 16" length of foil with the sesame oil.

Place the salmon on the foil to one side of its center. Sprinkle it with the soy sauce, gingerroot, garlic and sesame seeds.

Fold the foil over the fish; then fold and tightly crimp the edges together to form a D-shaped packet. Transfer the packet to the hot baking sheet, and bake for eight minutes.

On a dinner plate, slit open the packet's straight side and withdraw the foil, leaving the salmon and its juices on the plate. Spoon the snow peas over the fish.

Oven-Steamed Snow Peas

Place the snow peas in a shallow baking dish, and lightly season them with salt. Add the boiling water, and tightly cover the dish with foil. Bake at 425° for eight minutes, alongside the salmon, until tender-crisp.

Note: *Snow peas, an Asian bean with flat pods and tiny, immature peas inside, should be lightly cooked—pods and all—and eaten whole. They're available frozen, although the texture is far better when fresh. Sugar snap peas may be substituted.*

Salmon Fillet with Dill

with Oven-Steamed Red Potatoes

Salmon Fillet with Dill
one serving

- **Olive oil spray**
- **1 salmon fillet** (5 ounces)
- **Salt and pepper**
- **½ teaspoon chopped fresh dill**
- **2 lemon wedges**

Oven-Steamed Red Potatoes
one serving

- **4 small red potatoes** (4 ounces total), unpeeled and quartered
- **Olive oil spray**
- **Salt**
- **2 ice cubes**
- **Chopped parsley**

Salmon and feathery, bright green dill are a classic combination that comes off particularly well when cooked in a foil packet. Their flavors are concentrated, and the fish remains moist. Steamed in a separate foil packet, red potatoes make the perfect side dish.

Salmon Fillet with Dill

With a baking sheet in place, preheat the oven to 425°.

For each serving, spray the center area of a 16" length of foil with olive oil. Place the salmon on the foil, to one side of its center. Season it with salt and pepper to taste, and sprinkle with the dill.

Fold the foil over the fish; then fold and tightly crimp the edges together to form a D-shaped packet. Transfer the packet to the hot baking sheet, and bake for eight minutes.

On a dinner plate, slit open the packet's straight side and withdraw the foil, leaving the salmon on the plate. Serve with the lemon wedges for squeezing over the salmon.

Oven-Steamed Red Potatoes

For each serving, lightly spray a 16" length of foil with olive oil. Arrange the potatoes to one side of its center. Season with salt, and add the ice cubes. Fold the foil over the potatoes; then fold and tightly crimp the edges together to make a D-shaped packet. Transfer the packet to the hot baking sheet, and bake at 425° for 20 minutes.

Snip open the top of the packet, and spoon the potatoes onto a dinner plate. Sprinkle with parsley before serving.

Note: *When cooking the salmon and potatoes together, the potatoes should go into the hot oven about 12 minutes ahead of the fish. Both will be done at the same time.*

Nut-Crusted Salmon Fillet
with Yogurt "Mayonnaise" Sauce

Nut-Crusted Salmon Fillet
one serving

- **Olive oil spray**
- **1 salmon fillet** (5 ounces)
- **1 teaspoon olive oil**
- **1/8 teaspoon ground nutmeg** (preferably freshly grated)
- **Salt and pepper**
- **1/4 cup nuts** (walnuts or pecans), finely chopped

Yogurt "Mayonnaise" Sauce
1/2 cup (two servings)

- **1/2 cup plain yogurt** (low-fat or nonfat)
- **1 teaspoon Dijon mustard**
- **1 teaspoon olive oil**
- **1/4 teaspoon sugar**
- **1 1/2 teaspoons capers,** drained
- **1 1/2 teaspoons chopped parsley**

Although very simple to assemble, this is a sophisticated dish. The salmon's toasty nut coating contrasts with the smooth, tangy sauce, and all the flavors complement each other.

Nut-Crusted Salmon Fillet

With a baking sheet in place, preheat the oven to 425°.

For each serving, lightly spray the center of an 8" length of foil with olive oil. Then place the salmon on the foil, and brush it with the olive oil.

Season with the nutmeg, and salt and pepper to taste. Cover it with the chopped nuts, pressing them in evenly.

Using a broad metal spatula, transfer the fish on its foil to the hot baking sheet, using a broad metal spatula. Bake the fish for ten minutes.

Transfer the fish to a dinner plate, and serve with half the sauce spooned on one side.

Yogurt "Mayonnaise" Sauce

Spoon the yogurt into a small serving bowl. Add the mustard, olive oil and sugar; and stir until smooth. Then stir in the capers and parsley.

Note: *Preground nutmeg tends to quickly go stale; so for true flavor, grating whole nutmeg is recommended. (A rotary nutmeg grinder has one happy advantage over a grater: It will save your knuckles from being rasped by mistake.)*

Lemon Snapper
with Baked Tomatoes

Lemon Snapper
one serving

- **Olive oil spray**
- **1 red snapper fillet** (6 ounces)
- **Salt and pepper**
- **Juice of ½ lemon**
- **1 green onion** (including pale green leaves), chopped
- **1 tablespoon unsalted butter,** cut up
- **1 teaspoon capers,** drained
- **1 tablespoon dry white wine**
- **1 lemon wedge**

Baked Tomatoes
one serving

- **2 ripe Roma tomatoes,** cut in half lengthwise
- **4 black olives,** pitted and chopped
- **Pepper**

The Mediterranean combination of fresh lemon-flavored fish and Roma tomatoes with olives, capers and olive oil makes a thoroughly satisfying dish. (The tomatoes should begin baking five minutes before the fish.) Serve with a good, crusty bread and a simple wine.

Lemon Snapper

With a foil-lined baking sheet in place, preheat the oven to 425°.

For each serving, lightly spray the center area of an 18" length of foil with olive oil. Place the snapper to one side of the center of the foil. Season lightly with salt and pepper, and drizzle with the lemon juice. Top with the chopped green onion, butter and capers. Sprinkle with the wine.

Fold the foil over the fish; then fold and tightly crimp the edges together to form a D-shaped packet. Transfer the packet to the hot baking sheet, and bake for ten minutes.

On a dinner plate, slit open the packet's straight side and withdraw the foil, leaving the fish and sauce on the plate. Serve with the lemon wedge and baked tomato halves to the side.

Baked Tomatoes

For each serving, arrange the tomato halves on a foil-lined baking sheet; top with the olives, and season with pepper to taste. Bake at 425° in a preheated oven for 15 minutes.

Note: *If you're baking more than one serving and there's not enough room for everything on one baking sheet, bake the tomatoes first and set them aside until the fish are done. Then return them to the oven to warm while you arrange the fish on dinner plates.*

Boned Whole Trout
with Mushroom Sauce

Boned Whole Trout
one serving

- **1 tablespoon butter**
- **6 ounces brown or white mushrooms** (about 6), sliced
- **1 large shallot,** finely chopped
- **1 thin slice prosciutto** (1 ounce)
- **Salt and pepper**
- **1 tablespoon chopped parsley**
- **1 whole trout** (6 ounces), boned

A trout's finely grained, delicate meat tastes delicious when cooked in foil, especially when set off by the earthy flavor of mushrooms.

With a baking sheet in place, preheat the oven to 425°.

For each serving, have a 16" length of foil ready.

In a skillet, heat the butter, and sauté the mushrooms, shallot and prosciutto for one minute. Season lightly with salt and a generous grinding of pepper; then stir in the parsley.

Spoon one fourth of the mushroom sauce onto the foil, to one side of its center, and top it with the trout.

Spoon another one fourth of the mushroom sauce inside the trout, and spread what remains over the trout.

Fold the foil over the fish; then fold and tightly crimp the edges together to form a D-shaped packet. Transfer the packet to the hot baking sheet, and bake for ten minutes.

On a dinner plate, slit open the packet's straight side and withdraw the foil, leaving the trout and mushroom sauce on the plate.

Note: *Most recipes call for a very small quantity of fresh parsley. Rather than leave the rest of the bunch to wilt, rinse and dry it in a salad spinner, then chop and freeze it in a plastic tub (a recycled yogurt container is ideal) for use later on. Since well-dried chopped parsley won't freeze solid, it can be spooned out as needed.*

Baking

PROFESSIONAL BAKERS use parchment by the mile for lining baking sheets and cake pans, but the aluminum foil you already have can serve the same purpose. Like parchment, it prevents cakes and cookies from sticking to the pan. But that's only the beginning of the uses for foil in baking.

I've become a convert to fluted foil baking cups, which are rigid enough to stand unaided on a baking sheet. This allows several dozen cupcakes or muffins to be baked at the same time, and then there's no muffin tin to wash. Foil pie pans are invaluable, too, for making my favorite crusty flat breads, while cakes baked in inexpensive, disposable foil pans are easily transported or frozen for later.

Throughout this chapter, brown rice flour is listed as an alternative to all-purpose flour. Despite the many benefits of this cream-colored, whole-grain flour, it still seems to be a well-kept secret. I use quite a lot of it in baking, partly because it adds a mellow, nutty flavor to breads, cakes and cookies, and partly because it's so healthful. With its nutritious bran still intact, brown rice flour creates a far lighter crumb than whole wheat flour, and it's indispensable in recipes for delicate pastries. You'll find it at natural-foods stores and by mail order.

Quick Flat Breads

Made with Wheat Flour and Ground Almonds

Quick Flat Breads *(Wheat Flour)*
two 3/4-pound loaves

- **2 cups flour** (bread flour or all-purpose flour), plus additional
- **1/2 cup almonds**
- **1 1/2 teaspoons baking powder**
- **1 teaspoon baking soda**
- **1/2 teaspoon salt**
- **1/2 cup plain yogurt** (low-fat or nonfat)
- **1/2 cup water**
- **2 tablespoons mild vegetable oil**
- **1 large egg**

You'll be glad this recipe produces two loaves—and in so very little time. The very moist dough, which isn't kneaded, will rise as it bakes in the center of a simple foil pie pan. More akin to Italian focaccia *than to the usual baking powder breads, each loaf has a beautiful golden crust. Ground almonds add good flavor and texture.*

With a baking sheet in place, preheat the oven to 425°.

Lightly sprinkle the bottoms of two 9" foil pie pans with a little flour.

Using a food processor, combine one cup of the flour, the almonds, baking powder, baking soda and salt. Process until the almonds are finely ground. Then add the remaining one cup of flour, and process to mix.

In a bowl, mix the yogurt, water, oil and egg. Add to the flour mixture, and process until a soft, sticky dough forms.

Using a rubber spatula, mound half the dough in the center of each pan. Sprinkle with additional flour. To retain air in the dough, gently pat the dough flat, leaving a 2" perimeter around each pan. Sprinkle additional flour around the edges of the dough, and gently shape it into two 1/2" thick, 6 1/2" diameter loaves.

With a sharp knife, mark a diamond grid pattern on top of each loaf by pressing the blade 1/4" deep, three times one way and three times the other, wiping the blade clean after each cut.

Transfer the pans to the hot baking sheet, and bake until the loaves are golden brown and crusty, about 20 minutes. Remove the loaves from the pans, and let them cool on a wire rack.

Note: *See page 94 for flat breads baked with gluten-free brown rice flour and ground nuts.*

Quick Flat Breads

Made with Brown Rice Flour and Ground Nuts

Quick Flat Breads *(Brown Rice Flour)*
two 3/4-pound loaves

- **1 cup brown rice flour,** plus additional
- **1/2 cup nuts** *(see below)*
- **1/2 cup cornstarch** (or potato starch)
- **1 teaspoon baking powder**
- **1 teaspoon baking soda**
- **1/2 teaspoon salt**
- **1 1/2 teaspoons xanthan gum powder**
- **1/2 cup plain yogurt** (low-fat or nonfat)
- **1/2 cup water**
- **2 tablespoons mild vegetable oil**
- **1 large egg**

Almond Flat Breads
Use 1/2 cup almonds.

Hazelnut Flat Breads
Use 1/2 cup hazelnuts, plus one teaspoon unsweetened cocoa powder.

Walnut Flat Breads
Use 1/2 cup walnuts, and one egg white instead of one whole egg.

Good by any standard, these quickly made, crusty loaves are manna from heaven for anyone with an intolerance to wheat flour. One of the loaves can be frozen for later. (See page 93 for flat breads baked with wheat flour.)

With a baking sheet in place, preheat the oven to 425°.

Lightly sprinkle the bottoms of two 9" foil pie pans with a little brown rice flour.

Using a food processor, combine one cup of the rice flour, the nuts, cornstarch, baking powder, baking soda, salt and xanthan gum powder. Process until the nuts are finely ground.

In a bowl, mix the yogurt, water, oil and egg. Add to the flour mixture, and process until a soft, sticky dough forms.

Using a rubber spatula, mound half the dough in the center of each pan. Sprinkle with additional rice flour. To retain air in the dough, gently pat the dough flat, leaving a 2" perimeter around each pan. Sprinkle a little more flour around the edges of the dough, and gently shape it into two 1/2" thick, 6 1/2" diameter loaves.

With a sharp knife, mark a diamond grid pattern on top of each loaf by pressing the blade 1/4" deep, three times one way and three times the other, wiping the blade clean after each cut.

Transfer the pans to the hot baking sheet, and bake until the loaves are golden brown and crusty, about 20 minutes. Remove the loaves from the pans, and let them cool on a wire rack.

Note: *Available at natural-foods stores or by mail order (see Resources, page 125), xanthan gum powder is a carbohydrate derived from corn syrup—and the magic ingredient that facilitates baking with brown rice flour. Since the flour contains no gluten, xanthan gum is added to create elasticity. It may seem expensive, at one dollar per ounce, but a little goes a long way.*

Corn Muffins

Made with Pecans

Corn Muffins
12 muffins

- **1 cup yellow cornmeal**
- **1/4 cup chopped pecans**
- **1 cup all-purpose flour** (or brown rice flour)
- **1/2 cup cornstarch**
- **1/2 teaspoon salt**
- **1 tablespoon baking powder**
- **2 tablespoons sugar**
- **2 large eggs**
- **1 1/4 cups water**
- **4 tablespoons butter,** melted

Pairing corn with pecans strikes me as only natural since both are only native to the Americas. With their taste more savory than sweet, these tender muffins with bits of pecan make a good alternative to dinner rolls for practically any dinner.

Preheat the oven to 425°. Arrange 12 foil baking cups on a baking sheet, about 1/2" apart.

In a mixing bowl, combine the cornmeal, pecans, flour, cornstarch, salt, baking powder and sugar. Mix well.

In a separate bowl, beat the eggs, water and melted butter together with a fork. Pour over the dry ingredients and lightly blend. (The batter will be quite runny.) Fill each baking cup approximately three fourths full, and transfer the sheet and cups to the oven.

Bake about 15 minutes, until well risen and golden brown. A toothpick inserted in the center of a muffin should come out clean. Remove the muffins from the foil baking cups before serving them warm.

Note: *Pecans are harvested in the autumn, and that's a good time to buy them (or gather them, if you're so lucky). Like most nuts, they are high in beneficial fats, which eventually cause them to spoil. Unshelled, they'll keep for months, while shelled pecans should be stored in the freezer. Always sample one to be sure they're still fresh and sweet.*

Almond Biscotti

Flavored with Anise and Lemon

Almond Biscotti
18 cookies

- **1/3 cup whole almonds,** with skins
- **1/2 cup sugar**
- **4 tablespoons unsalted butter,** softened
- **1 large egg**
- **1 large egg yolk**
- **1/2 cup all-purpose flour** (or brown rice flour, see *Note*), plus additional
- **1/2 cup cornstarch** (or potato starch)
- **Pinch of salt**
- **1/4 teaspoon baking powder**
- **1 tablespoon anise seeds**
- **1 teaspoon grated lemon zest**

In Italian, biscottare *means "twice baked," and to the Italians, that can only mean biscotti—sweet, crunchy rusks meant for dipping in a glass of Vin Santo or espresso. Interestingly, biscotti were originally twice baked to ensure that they'd last throughout a long voyage. So you can be sure they'll keep for months in an airtight container; although as irresistible as they are, you'd be well advised to bake two batches.*

Preheat the oven to 300°.

In a food processor, combine the almonds and half the sugar, and process to a fine meal. Transfer to a small bowl and set aside.

In the food processor bowl, combine the remaining sugar and the butter, and process until light and creamy. Add the whole egg and the yolk, and process just long enough to blend. Add the reserved almond-sugar mixture, the flour, cornstarch, salt, baking powder, anise seeds and lemon zest. Process just long enough to form a crumbly dough.

On a lightly floured sheet of foil, shape the dough into a log-like roll about 10" long. (It will spread as it bakes.)

Transfer the foil with the dough to a baking sheet, and bake about 40 minutes, until pale golden brown.

Remove the log from the baking sheet, and let it cool on a rack. When cold, cut it on the diagonal into 1/2" wide slices, and lay them flat on the foil-lined baking sheet.

Bake at 300° for ten minutes; then turn each cookie over and bake another ten minutes, until they're crisp and dry throughout. Let them cool on a rack before serving.

Note: *If you substitute brown rice flour for all-purpose flour, you must add one teaspoon of xanthan gum powder with the other dry ingredients. Available at natural-foods stores or by mail order (see Resources, page 125), xanthan gum powder facilitates baking with brown rice flour.*

Greek Butter Cookies

Kourabiedes

Greek Butter Cookies
48 cookies

- **1 cup unsalted butter,** softened
- **3 tablespoons plus 2 cups confectioners' sugar**
- **1 egg yolk**
- **½ teaspoon almond extract**
- **½ cup sliced almonds,** lightly toasted, finely chopped and cooled
- **1½ cups brown rice flour**
- **½ cup cornstarch** (or potato starch)
- **Pinch of salt**
- **2 cups confectioners' sugar**

These melt-in-your-mouth cookies, known as kourabiedes, *are liberally coated with powdered sugar, so it's best to serve them in fluted baking cups (paper or foil) with the sides trimmed to an inch high. Amazed Greek friends have said they rival the cookies they remember from their mother's kitchen. The secret lies in the brown rice flour, which makes them so tender that they must be eaten in one bite.*

Preheat the oven to 325°.

Line two large baking sheets with foil.

Beat the butter until creamy, then beat in the three tablespoons of confectioners' sugar, the egg yolk, almond extract and almonds. In a separate bowl, combine the brown rice flour, cornstarch and salt; stir into the butter mixture. The dough will have a delicate consistency. (If it becomes too soft to handle, refrigerate the dough for a few minutes.)

Pinch off 1" diameter pieces of the dough, and gently roll them into balls between your palms. Place them 1" apart on the baking sheets, and refrigerate for ten minutes. Bake one sheet at a time, about 18 minutes, until the cookies turn pale golden brown.

Remove the baking sheet from the oven, and let the cookies cool on the sheet for five minutes. Sift one cup of the confectioners' sugar onto a large sheet of foil. With a metal spatula, transfer the warm cookies onto the sugar; then sift the remaining confectioners' sugar over the cookies, covering them completely. Let the cookies cool before serving in fluted baking cups.

Note: *These cookies may be frozen for up to one week; place them in a single layer in an airtight container.*

Almond Macaroons

Amaretti

Almond Macaroons
30 cookies

- **7 ounces pure almond paste,** chopped
- **½ cup granulated sugar**
- **2 egg whites,** lightly beaten
- **½ cup confectioners' sugar**
- **1 tablespoon all-purpose flour** (or brown rice flour)

A wonderful dessert cookie with sweet wine or coffee, these crunchy little round macaroons are easy to make, and they keep well if stored in an airtight container. To embellish a simple dessert of ice cream, crumble a couple of amaretti *and sprinkle them on top, then add fresh berries.*

Preheat the oven to 350°. Line a large baking sheet with foil, and prepare a pastry bag fitted with a ½" plain round tip.

In a food processor, combine the almond paste and the granulated sugar. Process until they're well mixed. Add the egg whites, and process until blended. Then add the confectioners' sugar and flour, and process until smooth.

Using a rubber spatula, transfer the mixture to the pastry bag. Pipe the dough in 1" diameter mounds onto the foil-lined sheet, about 1½" apart.

Using the back of a teaspoon dipped in water, smooth the peak of each cookie; then bake them for about 20 minutes, until light golden brown. Turn off the oven, and let the cookies dry out for another 30 minutes with the oven door partly open.

Transfer the cookies to a wire rack, and let them cool. Store in an airtight container to maintain their crispness.

Note: *Almond paste is a mixture of ground almonds and sugar. It is available at most specialty food stores, in the baking ingredients section of some supermarkets and by mail order (see Resources, page 125).*

Easy Pastry Shell
Made with Ground Almonds

Easy Pastry Shell
for one 9" pie or tart

- **½ cup whole almonds**
- **1 tablespoon sugar**
- **1 cup all-purpose flour** (or brown rice flour)
- **¼ cup cornstarch** (or potato starch)
- **½ cup cold butter,** cut up
- **1½ tablespoons cold water**

Easily made in a food processor, this meltingly tender pastry shell provides the ideal crust for the Almond Tart (page 100) and the Walnut-Prune Tart (page 101). By using a foil pie pan, you can prepare it in advance and keep it frozen, tightly wrapped, for up to two weeks.

In a food processor, combine the almonds and sugar, and process to a fine consistency.

Add the flour, cornstarch and butter; process to an even blend. Sprinkle with the cold water, and process briefly until the mixture holds together.

Remove the almond dough from the processor, and roll it between two sheets of plastic wrap into an 11" circle.

Peel away the top sheet of plastic, and flop the dough into a 9" foil pie pan. Then peel away the other sheet of plastic.

Trim the edges of the pastry shell, and patch if necessary with the dough trimmings (they won't be visible). Lightly press the tines of a fork around the rim.

Cool in the freezer for ten minutes before using.

Note: *The pastry shell may be baked without a filling at 350° for 25 minutes, until golden. Then allow it to cool before filling it with fruit, such as fresh berries or cooked apples.*

Almond Tart
with an Apricot-Lemon Glaze

Almond Tart
eight servings

- **Easy Pastry Shell** *(see page 99)*, unbaked and refrigerated, in a 9" foil pie pan
- **½ cup jam** (raspberry or lingonberry)
- **1 cup whole almonds**
- **½ cup sugar**
- **½ cup unsalted butter,** cut up and softened
- **2 large eggs**
- **2 tablespoons all-purpose flour** (or brown rice flour)

Apricot-Lemon Glaze

- **½ cup apricot jam**
- **½ cup confectioners' sugar,** sifted
- **2 tablespoons fresh lemon juice**

Swedish cooks are renowned for their wonderful pastries. This tart is very much like the one they call an Alexandertarta. *As it bakes, the almond filling turns into a soft nut sponge, hiding a layer of jam. The apricot and lemon glaze adds the finishing touch.*

Almond Tart

With a baking sheet in place, preheat the oven to 350°.

Gently spread the jam over the bottom of the cold, unbaked pastry shell.

In a food processor, process the almonds and sugar until finely ground. Blend in the butter. Then add the eggs, one at a time, and process until smooth. Add the flour, and process just long enough to mix.

With a spatula, spread the almond filling evenly over the jam.

Transfer the pan to the hot baking sheet, and bake 35 minutes, until golden brown. Supporting the pan from underneath, transfer the tart to a wire rack to cool (about one hour).

Apricot-Lemon Glaze

Melt the apricot jam over low heat, then strain it into a bowl. While still warm, brush it over the cool tart. Let it set, about one hour. Place the sugar in a small bowl, and stir in the lemon juice to make a translucent icing. (Add more lemon juice if it becomes too stiff to pour.) Immediately drizzle it over the apricot jam, and then spread with a pastry brush. It will harden almost at once.

Note: *Before serving the tart, slice it in the pan without cutting through the foil. Then place the slices on dessert plates or reassemble the tart on a serving platter for an impressive presentation. Unlike most tarts, this one can be refrigerated for two or three days without becoming soggy.*

Walnut-Prune Tart
with a Chocolate Glaze

Walnut-Prune Tart
eight to ten servings

- **Easy Pastry Shell** *(see page 99),* unbaked in a 9" foil pie pan
- **2½ cups soft pitted prunes**
- **1 cup dry white wine**
- **⅓ cup walnut pieces**
- **2 tablespoons sugar**
- **¾ cup sponge cake cubes,** in ½" cuts
- **2 tablespoons raisins**
- **1 tablespoon dried Zante currants,** rinsed and dried
- **Grated zest of 1 lemon**
- **3 tablespoons sherry**

Chocolate Glaze

- **3 ounces bittersweet chocolate,** chopped
- **1 tablespoon mild vegetable oil**

This tart is luxurious enough for a holiday dessert, but not overly sweet. If you haven't any leftover sponge cake, the sponge cake shells that are intended for holding berries and available at the supermarket will do.

Walnut-Prune Tart

In a small saucepan, simmer the prunes in the wine for 15 minutes, until soft. Then let them cool slightly.

With a baking sheet in place, preheat the oven to 375°.

Using a food processor, grind the walnuts and sugar to a coarse consistency. Transfer to a bowl and set aside. Then process the cake into crumbs, and add them to the walnuts.

Remove the prunes from the wine, and chop them in the food processor (being careful not to make a puree). Add the raisins, currants, walnut-cake mixture, lemon zest and sherry. Pulse just long enough to mix into a moist paste. (If it seems stiff, add some of the prune cooking liquid.)

Spoon the mixture into the pastry shell, transfer it to the hot baking sheet, and bake for 30 minutes. Carefully transfer the tart to a wire rack to cool (for about one hour).

Then evenly spread the Chocolate Glaze over it. Refrigerate until the chocolate sets (about 15 minutes). Serve at room temperature.

Chocolate Glaze

In a small bowl over hot water, melt the chocolate, stirring gently until completely smooth. Then stir in the vegetable oil.

Note: *When covering a tart or cake with a chocolate glaze, pour the chocolate on top, and then tilt the dessert to help the glaze spread evenly over the surface. Avoid using a spoon or brush, which would spoil the sheen of the chocolate once it sets.*

Simple Sponge Cake

Made in One Bowl

Simple Sponge Cake
eight servings

- **Cornmeal** (or brown rice flour)
- **1/2 cup unsalted butter,** softened
- **1/2 cup sugar**
- **2 large eggs**
- **1/2 teaspoon pure vanilla extract**
- **1/2 cup all-purpose flour** (or brown rice flour)
- **1/2 cup cornstarch** (or potato starch)
- **1 teaspoon baking powder**
- **Confectioners' sugar**

This delectable cake is easy to make and very versatile: Enjoy it plain or lightly dusted with confectioners' sugar, and serve it with fresh berries or the Spanish Apricot Compote on page 116. Even though all-purpose flour works well, brown rice flour results in an even more tender cake.

Preheat the oven to 350°.

Sprinkle the bottom of an 8" cake pan with a little cornmeal so the liner won't stick, and line it with a circle of foil *(see Techniques, page 11).*

Using an electric mixer, beat the butter and sugar until light and fluffy. Beat in the eggs, one at a time; then add the vanilla.

Sift the flour, cornstarch and baking powder over the butter mixture, and stir until smooth (the batter will be thick).

Transfer the batter to the cake pan, and level it with a spatula. Bake for 28 minutes, until the cake is golden and shrinks away slightly from the sides.

Let it rest for five minutes. Loosen the cake by gently running a knife around its perimeter. Unmold it onto a flat plate, and gently remove the pan and the foil. Place a wire cake rack over the cake and reverse both, so the cake is upright again. Let it cool on the rack. Then lightly dust with confectioners' sugar before serving.

Note: *Use leftover sponge cake in the recipe for Walnut-Prune Tart on page 101.*

Chocolate Brownie Cake

Made without Eggs

Chocolate Brownie Cake
nine servings

- **Vegetable oil**
- **1/2 cup all-purpose flour** (or brown rice flour)
- **1/2 cup cornstarch** (or potato starch)
- **3 tablespoons unsweetened cocoa powder**
- **Pinch of salt**
- **1/2 teaspoon baking powder**
- **1/2 cup ground almonds**
- **1 cup sugar**
- **6 tablespoons mild vegetable oil**
- **1 1/2 teaspoons apple cider vinegar**
- **3/4 cup water**
- **Confectioners' sugar**

Although it has the rich, fudgy taste of a brownie, this cake contains neither butter nor eggs—and is cholesterol free. Don't overlook the touch of cider vinegar, which helps the cake to rise.

Preheat the oven to 350°.

Lightly grease an 8" square foil cake pan with oil, and place it on a baking sheet.

Sift the flour, cornstarch, cocoa, salt and baking powder into a mixing bowl. Stir in the ground almonds and sugar.

Combine the vegetable oil, vinegar and water. Pour this over the flour mixture, and stir until the batter is smooth. (It will be quite runny.)

Pour the batter into the cake pan. Transfer the baking sheet and cake to the oven. Bake for 30 minutes, until the cake is firm and a toothpick inserted in the center of it comes out clean.

Transfer the cake pan to a wire rack, and let the cake cool until lukewarm. Then dust it with confectioners' sugar. Cut it into squares, and serve warm or at room temperature.

Note: *As an alternative to dusting the cake with confectioners' sugar, give it a rich Chocolate Glaze (see page 101). After the cake is completely cool in the pan, pour the glaze over it, and refrigerate until the glaze has set, about 15 minutes.*

Chocolate-Hazelnut Torte

Torta di Noce

Chocolate-Hazelnut Torte
ten servings

- **Butter**
- **Cornmeal** (or brown rice flour)
- **1½ cups chopped hazelnuts**
- **4 ounces bittersweet or semisweet chocolate,** coarsely chopped
- **1 ounce unsweetened chocolate**
- **5 large eggs**
- **⅔ cup sugar**
- **1 teaspoon pure vanilla extract**
- **1 tablespoon all-purpose flour** (or brown rice flour)
- **1 tablespoon cornstarch** (or potato starch)
- **Confectioners' sugar**

The basis for this low-rising cake (1½" to 2" high) is torta di noce, *a traditional Italian cake. In adapting the almost flour-free recipe, I've substituted hazelnuts for the usual walnuts.*

Preheat the oven to 350°.

Coat the sides of a 9" diameter cake pan with butter. Sprinkle the bottom with a little cornmeal so the liner won't stick, and line it with a circle of foil *(see Techniques, page 11).*

Using a nut mill or clean coffee grinder, pulverize the hazelnuts and chocolates in several small batches to the fine consistency of flour. (A food processor would produce heavy granules that prevent the cake from rising properly.) Combine them and set aside.

In a mixing bowl, combine the eggs and sugar. Using an electric mixer, beat until pale and very thick, five or six minutes. A slowly dissolving ribbon should fall from the beaters when lifted. Then beat in the vanilla.

Sift the flour and cornstarch over the batter, and fold it in. Then fold in the hazelnut-chocolate mixture, deflating the batter as little as possible. Pour the batter into the pan, and smooth the top.

Bake 40 minutes, until a toothpick inserted in the center of the cake comes out clean.

Let the cake rest for five minutes. Unmold onto a flat plate, and gently remove the pan and foil. Place a wire cake rack over the cake and reverse both, so the cake is upright again. Let it cool on the rack. Dust with confectioners' sugar before serving.

Note: *It is normal for an almost flour-free cake to sink very slightly in the middle. An 8" springform pan can be substituted for the 9" cake pan; its high sides will easily accommodate the batter.*

Gingerbread

An Old Holiday Cake

Gingerbread
nine servings

- **Vegetable oil**
- **4 tablespoons unsalted butter,** softened
- **¼ cup sugar**
- **1 large egg**
- **½ cup dark molasses**
- **1¼ cups all-purpose flour** (or brown rice flour)
- **¼ cup cornstarch** (or potato starch)
- **1 teaspoon baking powder**
- **1 teaspoon ground ginger**
- **¼ teaspoon ground allspice**
- **¼ teaspoon ground cloves**
- **⅛ teaspoon salt**
- **⅔ cup low-fat milk**

With its friendly aroma, gingerbread has a long history as a dessert. And like Scottish shortbread, it was never a bread, but always a special treat.

Preheat the oven to 350°.

Lightly grease an 8" square foil cake pan with vegetable oil, and place it on a baking sheet.

Using an electric mixer, beat the butter and sugar together until light and fluffy. Beat in the egg and molasses. In a separate bowl, combine the flour, cornstarch, baking powder, ginger, allspice, cloves and salt. Add to the butter-sugar mixture alternately with the milk, beating well after each addition.

Pour the batter into the cake pan. Transfer the baking sheet and pan to the oven. Bake for 30 minutes, until the cake is firm and a toothpick inserted in the center of it comes out clean.

Cool in the pan on a wire rack. Cut into squares, and serve warm or at room temperature.

Note: *Many baking spices have a way of sitting in the pantry from one holiday season to the next, growing ever fainter in flavor. Do remember to replace them at least once a year, and preferably more often.*

Orange Cupcakes

Made with Orange Juice

Orange Cupcakes
nine cupcakes

- **½ cup orange juice**
- **1 large egg**
- **2 tablespoons mild vegetable oil**
- **2 tablespoons sugar**
- **Grated zest of ½ orange**
- **¾ cup all-purpose flour** (or brown rice flour)
- **¼ cup cornstarch** (or potato starch)
- **1 teaspoon baking powder**
- **½ teaspoon baking soda**
- **¼ teaspoon salt**

With orange juice as a substitute for water or milk, these extra-light cupcakes have a wonderful citrus flavor. Any leftovers can be saved for breakfast the next morning, or frozen for later.

Preheat the oven to 425°.

Arrange nine foil baking cups on a baking sheet, about 1" apart.

In a mixing bowl, beat the orange juice, egg, oil, sugar and orange zest with a fork until smooth.

Stir in the flour, cornstarch, baking powder, baking soda and salt. Beat just long enough to make a fairly smooth batter.

Fill each baking cup approximately three fourths full, and transfer the sheet and cups to the oven. Bake 12 minutes, until a toothpick inserted in the center of a cupcake comes out clean.

Transfer the foil cups to a wire rack to cool. Serve the cupcakes warm or at room temperature.

Note: *If your cupcakes turn out dense and less than tender, it's usually because the batter has been beaten too long. Keep in mind that the batter doesn't have to be perfectly smooth.*

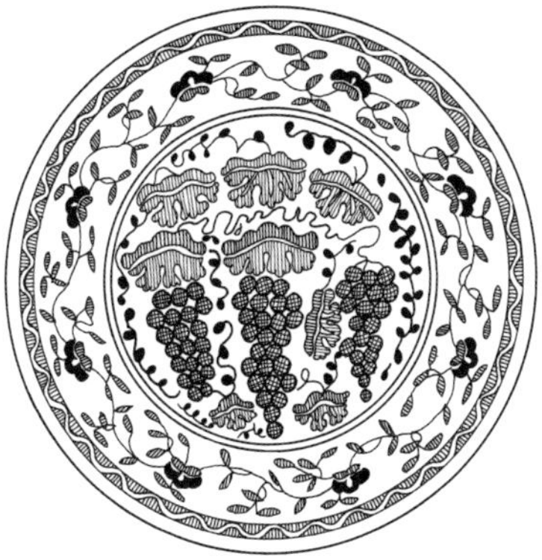

Desserts

AS THE EARLIEST-RECORDED DESSERT, fresh fruit afforded a cool, light, sweet complement to the savory main course, long before anyone imagined baking fruit in pastry and freezing sweetened cream, or extracted chocolate from the cacao bean.

I have a weakness for warm fruit desserts served with ice cream or yogurt on the side; the blend of hot and cold, sweet and slightly tart is enticing. While preassembled foil packets of buttery, caramelized apple slices are busily baking, I can enjoy lingering over the main course.

Serving ice cream at the end of a meal became an American tradition from the time Thomas Jefferson introduced it to his dinner guests, one of whom wrote: "The ice cream was brought to the table in the form of small balls, enclosed in cases of warm pastry, a feat."

To make an ice cream dessert more special (the Jeffersonian technique does sound rather daunting), I serve it in chocolate scallop shells. Covering the natural shells with foil, painting on thin layers of melted chocolate and then easing the chilled chocolate shells off their molds takes a little time and patience at first, but the result is worth the effort. (You'll find other recipes for desserts in the chapter on baking.)

Chocolate Scallop Shells

with Ice Cream and Raspberry Sauce

Chocolate Scallop Shells
four servings

- **6 ounces bittersweet chocolate**, finely chopped
- **4 scoops vanilla ice cream**
- **2 cups Raspberry Sauce**
- **Fresh raspberries and mint leaves**

Raspberry Sauce
one cup

- **2 cups raspberries** (fresh or frozen)
- **2 tablespoons raspberry jam**
- **2 tablespoons water**
- **Sugar** (optional)

In a food processor, blend the raspberries (reserving some for the garnish), jam and water, then strain the mixture into a bowl. Add sugar to taste, if needed. (If the sauce is too thick to pour, stir in a little water.) Refrigerate until ready to serve.

These delicate chocolate shells look stunning and, of course, taste delicious. To make them, you'll need natural scallop shells, aluminum foil and a clean, dry pastry brush. I've found that brushing on two thin coats of chocolate results in a stronger shell than a single thick coat. As an alternative to raspberry sauce, add sliced bananas, walnuts and chocolate sauce, or cold baked apricots and butterscotch sauce.

Line a baking sheet with foil. Cover the back of four scallop shells with enough foil to smoothly mold between the ribbing of the shell's surface and wrap over its edges, with extra foil tucked under.

Melt the chocolate over hot water. Then, holding each shell by its rounded edge, paint a thin layer of chocolate over the foil to within 3/4" of the rounded edge. Arrange the shells, chocolate-side up, on the baking sheet, and refrigerate for 15 minutes, until the chocolate hardens.

Repeat, giving each shell a second coating. (If the chocolate in the bowl has thickened, warm the bowl over hot water.) Then return the shells to the refrigerator for 30 minutes.

To unmold, release the foil from the underside of each shell, and ease the chocolate-coated foil off the shell. Then, very gently peel the foil from the chocolate, a little at a time. Trim the uneven rounded edge with scissors. Lay the chocolate shells curved-side up on the baking sheet, and refrigerate (up to 24 hours) before serving.

To serve, place the chocolate shells on chilled dessert plates, fill each with a small scoop of ice cream, and top with raspberry sauce. Garnish with fresh raspberries and mint leaves.

Note: *Unless you're a beachcomber with your own supply of shells, you'll find natural scallop shells with a diameter of no more than 5" available at many specialty cookware stores (see Resources, page 125). They're typically used for baking and serving Coquilles St. Jacques and other baked seafood dishes.*

Chocolate-Mocha Truffles

A Refrigerated Confection

Chocolate-Mocha Truffles
about 48 truffles

- **1 cup heavy cream** (8 ounces)
- **1 cup unsalted butter,** cut up
- **8 ounces bittersweet chocolate,** coarsely chopped
- **1 tablespoon instant espresso coffee**
- **1 tablespoon dark rum**
- **Unsweetened cocoa powder**

Preparation
To line the 8" square pan, fold each long side of a 20" length of foil under to reduce its width enough to completely cover the bottom of the pan. Center the foil in the pan so that it covers and overhangs two opposite ends, leaving the two sides uncovered. Tuck the loose ends of the foil under the pan to use later as handles for loosening the chocolate block in the pan.

So simple to make, these delicious little truffles provide a perfect ending to the perfect dinner.

In a medium saucepan, bring the cream and the butter to a boil. Remove from the heat, add the chocolate and coffee granules, and stir until melted. Then stir in the rum.

Partially line an 8" square cake pan with foil *(see Preparation),* and pour the chocolate mixture through a fine strainer into the pan. Let it cool; then cover the pan with another sheet of foil, and freeze for six hours.

Sift a generous layer of cocoa onto a sheet of foil.

To unmold the chocolate: Remove the foil cover from the pan, and loosen the sides of the chocolate block by gently pulling the loose foil upward. Then turn the pan upside down over the cocoa. The block of chocolate should slide out. Carefully peel the foil from its bottom and sides.

Sift more cocoa on top of the chocolate. Then, using a long, straight-edged knife, cut the chocolate in both directions, forming squares or diamonds. Separate the pieces, place them in individual foil candy cups, and store in the refrigerator.

Note: *These truffles should be kept refrigerated and eaten within three or four days to ensure their best flavor and texture.*

Chestnut Truffle Cake

A Refrigerated Dessert

Chestnut Truffle Cake
12 servings

- **6 ounces bittersweet chocolate,** finely chopped
- **2 ounces unsweetened baking chocolate,** finely chopped
- **3/4 cup unsalted butter**, softened
- **3/4 cup sugar**
- **15½-ounce can French chestnut puree,** cut in chunks
- **Pinch of salt**
- **Zest of 1 small orange,** grated
- **3 tablespoons brandy**
- **Confectioners' sugar**
- **1/4 cup finely chopped crystallized ginger**

An English holiday specialty at Lavenham Farm in Suffolk, which was owned by my dear friends Mary and Roger Wheeler for many years, this giant truffle is simply mixed and chilled, without baking. I recommend using a food processor rather than an electric mixer to blend the ingredients—with a mixer, the cake's texture won't be quite so silky. Be sure to use the best-quality chocolate. Serve the cake sliced like a savory pâté.

Smoothly line a rectangular loaf pan with foil. *(See Techniques, page 11.)*

Over hot water, melt the bittersweet and unsweetened chocolate together, stirring occasionally. Then let them cool to lukewarm.

Place the butter and sugar in a food processor, and process until smooth and fluffy. Blend in the chestnut puree, one third at a time. Then add the melted chocolate, salt, orange zest and brandy. Process until the mixture is very smooth.

Pour the mixture into the the foil-lined pan, and smooth the top. Cover the pan tightly with another piece of foil, pressing it gently against the surface of the cake, and refrigerate for at least four hours.

To unmold, remove the foil cover, loosen the sides of the cake with a knife, and invert a flat serving plate over the loaf pan. Then reverse the plate and pan. Carefully peel away the foil.

Cut the cake in 3/4" slices. On dessert plates, lightly dust each slice with confectioners' sugar, and sprinkle with a teaspoon of the crystallized ginger.

Note: *There is no substitute for chestnut puree, which you'll find at natural-foods stores and well-stocked supermarkets. Unlike other nuts and their pastes, chestnuts and chestnut puree contain no oil.*

Caramelized Apple Slices
with Ice Cream

Caramelized Apple Slices
one serving

- **1 medium apple** (Golden Delicious, Gala or Fuji)
- **1 tablespoon butter**
- **1 tablespoon sugar**
- **1 tablespoon dark rum**
- **1 tablespoon golden raisins**
- **1 tablespoon apricot jam**
- **1 scoop vanilla ice cream** (or plain yogurt)

These translucent, golden apple slices are served in a rum-flavored caramel sauce. Of course, they could be eaten right after being sautéed, but baking them in a foil packet lets the flavors develop fully, and allows you to serve the dessert at your convenience.

With a baking sheet in place, preheat the oven to 400°.

Peel and core the apple, and slice it into 12 wedges.

In a skillet, melt the butter. Add the apple wedges, sprinkle them with the sugar and sauté over medium-high heat, turning each wedge once, until they begin to caramelize, about seven minutes. Add the rum, and gently shake the pan over the burner until the liquid has almost evaporated. Then, add the raisins, and remove the pan from the heat.

For each serving, arrange the apple mixture on a 16" length of foil, to one side of its center. Top it with the jam.

Fold the foil over the apple wedges; then fold and tightly crimp the edges together to form a D-shaped packet. Transfer the packet to the hot baking sheet, and bake for ten minutes.

On a dessert plate, slit open the packet's straight side and withdraw the foil, leaving the apple wedges and sauce on the plate. Serve warm, with the ice cream on the side.

Note: *The packets can be prepared in advance and allowed to stand at room temperature for up to two hours; otherwise, they should be refrigerated and brought to room temperature before baking.*

Baked Banana
with Ice Cream

Baked Banana
one serving

- **1 tablespoon apricot jam**
- **1 tablespoon golden raisins**
- **1 tablespoon crystallized ginger,** thinly sliced
- **1 tablespoon dark rum**
- **1 medium ripe banana,** sliced diagonally into quarters
- **1 scoop vanilla ice cream** (or plain yogurt)

This dessert can be prepared in its packet ahead of time, then slipped into the oven after the main course. The scoop of vanilla ice cream on top will melt voluptuously into the warm sauce.

Preheat the oven to 375°.

For each serving, spoon the jam onto a 16" length of foil, to one side of its center. Top it with the raisins, ginger and rum. Gently roll the banana pieces in the mixture.

Fold the foil over the banana pieces; then fold and tightly crimp the edges together to form a D-shaped packet. Transfer the packet to a baking sheet, and bake for ten minutes.

On a dessert plate, slit open the packet's straight side and withdraw the foil, leaving the banana slices and sauce on the plate. Serve warm, topped with the ice cream.

Note: *When I plan to serve my guests a warm dessert, to ensure that it is warm and not overcooked, I serve a green salad after the main course, just as the French do. This allows enough time to bake a dessert from start to finish in foil packets.*

Baked Pear
with Chocolate Sauce

Baked Pear
one serving

- **½ tablespoon unsalted butter**
- **1 firm, ripe pear** (Comice or Bartlett)
- **1 ounce bittersweet chocolate**
- **1 tablespoon chopped walnuts,** toasted
- **1 scoop vanilla ice cream** (optional)

A variation on the classic Poire Belle Hélène, *this combination of warm fruit, dark chocolate and toasted walnuts is irresistible—and even more so with a scoop of vanilla ice cream. Once you've prepared the packet, it can be set aside for up to one hour before going into the oven.*

Preheat the oven to 375°.

For each serving, smear the center area of a 12" length of foil with the butter.

Peel the pear, and cut it in half. To keep each half level, cut a thin slice from its underside. With a teaspoon or melon baller, remove the core, and make a shallow well in the center of each half.

Arrange the two halves on the foil, side by side, both to one side of the center of the foil. Place half the chocolate in each well.

Fold the foil over the pear halves; then fold and tightly crimp the edges together to form a D-shaped packet. Place the packet on a baking sheet, and bake for ten minutes.

On a dessert plate, slit open the packet's straight side and withdraw the foil, leaving the pear halves on the plate. Sprinkle the walnut pieces on top of the melted chocolate. If desired, serve with a scoop of vanilla ice cream to one side of the pears.

Note: *A vegetable peeler does as good a job of peeling pears and apples as a paring knife, and most often in half the time.*

Baked Rhubarb and Apples
in Honey Syrup

Baked Rhubarb and Apples
four servings

- **1 tablespoon butter,** softened
- **1 pound rhubarb,** trimmed and cut in 1" pieces
- **½ pound apples** (Golden Delicious or Fuji), peeled and cut in ¾" cubes
- **6 tablespoons sugar**
- **6 tablespoons honey**
- **Whipped cream** (or plain yogurt)

Though generally regarded as a fruit, rhubarb is technically a vegetable. Until the eighteenth century, it was valued only for its medicinal properties, but then some inventive cook realized that the tart stalks are truly delicious simmered with sugar or honey. Look for fairly thick red or pink stalks without soft spots. (Discard the green leaves; their high acid content makes them toxic.) Rhubarb will fall apart if cooked too fast, but keeps its shape well when gently baked under foil.

Preheat the oven to 350°.

Grease a large baking dish with the butter, and arrange the rhubarb and apple pieces in it, in one layer. Sprinkle them with the sugar and drizzle with the honey *(see Note).*

Tightly cover the baking dish with foil, and bake for 30 minutes. Let it cool and then refrigerate.

Serve chilled, with a dollop of whipped cream, or as a sauce over plain yogurt.

Note: *To accurately add small quantities of honey, use a measuring spoon with its bowl lightly coated on both sides with soft butter. Every drop of the honey will slide off the spoon.*

Spanish Apricot Compote
Flavored with Amontillado Sherry

Spanish Apricot Compote
four to six servings

- **1 cup soft dried apricots**
- **3/4 cup soft, pitted prunes**
- **1/4 cup sugar**
- **1/2 cup amontillado sherry**
- **1 cinnamon stick**
- **6 whole cloves**
- **3 strips orange zest,** each cut 1" x 3"
- **1 1/2 cups boiling water**

The combination of tart apricots and sweet prunes is tantalizing. Fortified wines like sherry and port transform the two dried fruits into a wintertime treat, full flavored and rich tasting. Usually enjoyed as a before-dinner wine, amontillado is a Spanish sherry with a nutty flavor. It adds incomparable flavor to cooked foods. As a rule, cook with wines of the same quality as those you'd want to drink. Cream sherry, a sweet after-dinner sherry, may be used instead, but never settle for "cooking sherry."

Preheat the oven to 400°.

In a one-quart (four-cup) baking dish, combine the apricots, prunes, sugar, sherry and cinnamon stick.

Press the cloves through the strips of orange zest, and arrange them on top of the fruit.

Add the boiling water, and tightly cover the baking dish with foil. Bake for 25 minutes.

Before serving, remove and discard the cinnamon stick, orange zest and cloves. Serve lukewarm or chilled.

Note: *Baking this compote of dried fruits alongside whatever else you're cooking makes the most of the oven. For further efficiency, bake and serve it in the same baking dish.*

Sugarplums

A Holiday Confection

Sugarplums
40 sugarplums

- **¾ cup whole almonds**
- **6 tablespoons plus 1 cup sugar**
- **1 cup soft dried cranberries**
- **½ cup raisins**
- **½ cup soft, pitted prunes**
- **2 tablespoons honey**
- **1 teaspoon grated orange zest**
- **4 teaspoons brandy**

True sugarplums—whole glacéed green plums of a special wild variety—are still made in Portugal in a complex process that takes several days. But with a food processor, you can prepare your own delectable sugarplums from dried fruits in only half an hour. A must during the holiday season and a delicious after-dinner sweet anytime, they'll keep for at least two weeks if refrigerated in an airtight container.

In a food processor, combine the almonds and the six tablespoons of sugar, and process until finely ground.

Add the cranberries, raisins, prunes, honey and orange zest. Process until evenly ground.

Then add the brandy, and process into a smooth mixture that coheres well enough to be shaped.

Spread the one cup of sugar on a large sheet of foil. Form the fruit mixture into 1" diameter balls, and roll them in the sugar.

Serve in individual foil candy cups.

Note: *When finely chopping or grinding nuts in a food processor, adding the sugar in the recipe prevents the oily nuts from turning into a nut butter. The sugar left over after coating the sugarplums can be stored separately and used in baking.*

Tortoni

A Frozen Gâteau

Tortoni
nine servings

- **3/4 cup hazelnuts**
- **1½ cups heavy cream** (12 ounces)
- **½ cup confectioners' sugar**
- **3 tablespoons dark rum**
- **1½ cups amaretti crumbs**
- **9 ripe strawberries** (optional)

Preparation
To line the 8" square pan, fold each long side of a 20" length of foil under to reduce its width enough to completely cover the bottom of the pan. Center the foil in the pan so it covers and overhangs two opposite sides, leaving the other two uncovered. (The loose ends of the foil will be folded over the Tortoni.)

This sumptuous dessert has a long history. The Café Tortini was one of the most celebrated restaurants in nineteenth-century Paris. Its Italian owner was an ice cream maker as well as a chef, and his signature dessert lives on—and is far easier to make now than it was in 1830!

Preheat the oven to 350°. On a foil-lined baking sheet, toast the nuts for ten minutes, until fragrant and golden. Roll them in a clean kitchen towel to remove as much of their skins as possible. Then chop coarsely, and put them aside to cool.

Whip the cream until it starts to stiffen, then sift the sugar on top. Continue whipping until the sugar is incorporated and the cream is just stiff, but not dry looking. Then stir in the nuts and rum.

Partially line an 8" square cake pan with foil *(see Preparation),* and cover the foil with half the amaretti crumbs in an even layer. Spoon the cream mixture over the crumbs, then smooth it with a rubber spatula. Top with the remaining crumbs. Fold the loose foil ends over the top, gently pressing it to make a flat, even surface. Freeze for at least four hours.

To unmold, peel back the foil on top, and gently pull the two ends upward to loosen the frozen dessert. Invert a flat serving plate over the pan, then reverse the plate and pan. Carefully peel away the foil from the two ends and the bottom.

Cut the tortoni into squares (it won't have frozen hard) and, if desired, garnish each square with a strawberry.

Note: *Amaretti are crunchy little Italian macaroons made with almonds, sugar and egg whites. Some specialty food stores offer them, usually individually wrapped in tissue paper, or you may bake your own (see page 98).*

Notes

THE PERFECT DINNER starts with a plan. But many friends who enjoy cooking have confessed that dinner usually starts with confusion over what to serve with what. Like a satisfying story, a dinner menu has a beginning to set the tone, a middle that is most often its reason for being, and an ending that brings everything to a graceful, lingering close.

The cook's cardinal rules for planning a menu are simple: Cook the foods you like, build the menu around the freshest foods of the season, and avoid using any main ingredient more than once. With all that in mind, I've composed a menu of dinners from recipes that complement each other in terms of preparation and flavors. I hope they will at least provide the inspiration for you to create your own version of a perfect dinner.

Living in San Francisco, which is a cook's paradise, I sometimes too easily assume that the ingredients I use so casually are familiar—and readily available—across the country. The day will come when your local grocer will offer prosciutto and wedges of Parmigiano-Reggiano from Italy and brown rice flour you can scoop from a bin, but until then you may have to settle for satisfactory substitutes, or else order these special ingredients by mail. (It's usually well worth the wait and expense.)

Menus

"I never eat when I can dine." —Maurice Chevalier

Vegetarian

Corn and Black Bean Salad (page 26)
Asparagus Risotto (42)
Orange Cupcakes with Fresh Fruit (106)

Bell Pepper Soup (21)
Garlic-Flavored White Beans (72)
Steamed Broccoli Florets (24)
Warm Corn Muffins with Pecans (95)
Caramelized Apple Slices (112)

Zucchini Provençal (33)
Stuffed Portabella Mushrooms (28)
Toasted Brown Rice (41)
Italian-Style Broccoli Stems (24)
Chocolate Brownie Cake (103)

Chicken

Almond-Zucchini Appetizer (20)
Curried Chicken and Rice (55)
Fresh Fruit

Crumbed Chicken Breast (48)
Roasted Zucchini (48) and Herbed New Potatoes (30)
Green Salad
Baked Bananas with Ice Cream (113)

Portabella "Pizza" Appetizer (28)
Chicken Breast Cacciatore (47)
Warm Flat Bread (93)
Green Salad
Walnut Prune Tart (101)

Deviled Chicken Legs (50)
Oven-Steamed Red Potatoes (86)
Green Salad
Gingerbread (105)

Bell Pepper Soup (21)
Chicken Breast in Chard (49)
Rice Pilaf (40)
Chocolate Scallop Shells filled with
Ice Cream and Raspberry Sauce (109)

Diced Vegetable Salad (23)
Persian-Style Roast Chicken with
Dried Fruit Stuffing (58–59)
Rice Pilaf (40)
Chocolate-Mocha Truffles (110)

Lentil Salad (27) and Warm Flat Bread (93)
Roasted Chicken Legs with
Spinach-Almond Stuffing (56)
Buttered Asparagus (17)
Almond Macaroons (98) with Fresh Fruit

Meats

Filet Mignon with Mushroom Sauce (68)
Oven-Fried Potato Wedges (31)
Green Salad
Almond Biscotti with Fresh Fruit (96)

Warm Corn Muffins with Pecans (95)
Ham Steak and Green Peas (73)
Oven-Steamed Red Potatoes (86)
Fresh Fruit

Cold Asparagus Balsamico (18)
Roasted Pork Loin with Pine Nuts (74)
Buttered Radishes (32)
Green Salad
Tortoni (118)

Buttered Asparagus with Lemon (17)
Roasted Lamb Chops and White Beans (72)
Salad Greens
Caramelized Apple Slices with Ice Cream (112)

Seafood

Fresh Ahi Tuna Salad (79) and Warm Flat Bread (93)
Spanish Apricot Compote (116)

Bell Pepper Soup (21)
Nut-Crusted Salmon with Yogurt Sauce (87)
Green Salad
Warm Flat Bread (93)
Baked Pears with Chocolate (114)

Asparagus Risotto (42)
Lemon Snapper with Baked Tomatoes (88)
Chocolate-Hazelnut Torte (104)

Asian Zucchini Appetizer (20)
Bay Scallops with Roasted Bell Pepper (80)
Spicy Golden Rice (39)
Gingerbread (105)

Crispy Eggplant Appetizer (19)
Sea Bass with Buttered Leeks (83)
Spicy Golden Rice (39)
Sponge Cake with Fresh Berries (102)

Celebrations

Bell Pepper Soup (21)
Warm Flat Bread (93)
Roast Turkey and Gravy, with
Brown Rice and Sausage Stuffing (62)
Buttered Baby Carrots (25)
Diced Vegetable Salad (23)
Chestnut Truffle Cake (111)
Sugarplums (117)

Bell Pepper Appetizer (23)
Warm Flat Bread (93)
Crown Roast of Lamb with
Rice and Eggplant Stuffing (70)
Roasted Asparagus (18)
Green Salad
Baked Rhubarb and Apples in
Honey Syrup served over Yogurt (115)
Greek Butter Cookies (97)

Glossary
Ingredients

Balsamic Vinegar
True balsamic vinegar is produced only by the members of a consortium in Modena, Italy. Aging anywhere from two to 25 years in wooden barrels accounts for its dark color and rich, almost sweet flavor. A good balsamic vinegar is understandably expensive, but a little goes a long way. No other vinegar can substitute for it.

Bread Crumbs
The recipes in this cookbook call for soft white bread crumbs, which are quite different from the packaged variety. To make them: Remove the crusts from a slice of day-old white bread, and finely chop what remains with a knife or food processor. To keep a supply on hand, freeze the crumbs in an airtight container.

Brown Rice Flour
Milled from brown rice with its healthful bran intact, this cream-colored whole-grain flour is high in nutrients and fiber. It has a mellow flavor all its own. In most baking, it must be paired with *xanthan gum powder* to replace its missing gluten. (Silky white Asian rice flour is altogether different, and its primary use is as a thickener.) Store brown rice flour in the refrigerator or freezer. It is available at most natural-foods stores and by mail order.

Butter
Margarine and light butter are never adequate substitutes for real butter. It not only adds flavor to foods but also aids in browning. Fresh unsalted butter is your best choice for baking. (Salt is only added to butter as a preservative.)

Cheeses
James Beard once said that cheese "endears itself to everything." There are hundreds of varieties and many times that many uses. Always select wedges cut from a whole cheese, and buy only what you'll use immediately. A wedge of cheese will keep longer when it's tightly wrapped in foil rather than plastic wrap. (Plastic wrap causes it to sweat and become oily.) When a hard cheese begins to dry out, it can be grated, loosely packed in an airtight container, and refrigerated or frozen for use later.

California cheesemakers produce *Dry Jack* by aging their semisoft Monterey Jack up to 15 months. The result is a full-flavored hard cheese for grating and eating.

Feta is a soft, white cheese that originated in Greece. Its somewhat salty taste goes well with olives and in salads. You'll find it preserved in brine or vacuum-packed.

A semihard Swiss cheese speckled with small holes, *Gruyère* has a smooth texture and slightly sweet, nutty taste. It is versatile enough to be widely used in cooking (it melts well) and also enjoyed as a dessert cheese.

Parmesan is the anglicized name we gave to *Parmigiano-Reggiano,* a hard Italian cheese. Its salty, complex flavor and crumbly texture are the result of aging for two years or longer. The classic grating cheese for pastas, risottos and other dishes, Parmesan is best bought by the piece. There is no substitute for a wedge of imported Parmesan, which is a world apart from the familiar American grated Parmesan sold in shakers.

Pecorino refers to several types of hard Italian cheeses made from ewe's milk. (*Romano* is the best known variety.) It has a sharp, dry flavor.

Chicken
An *organic* or *free-range chicken* is well worth the added expense. Because the birds mature as nature intended (without hormones to speed their growth), they have a more flavorful meat with far less fat. Otherwise, look for fresh, unfrozen poultry.

Chocolate
There is no comparison between dark confectioner's chocolate and the supermarket variety. The distinction lies in the proportions of chocolate liquor, cocoa butter and sugar in their blends. Use the best chocolate available, and you'll appreciate the difference it makes in handling and taste. Valrhona, Callebaut and Lindt are European chocolates with well-deserved reputations; Scharffen Berger is a very fine American chocolate to look for.

To melt chocolate without a double boiler, I float a small metal bowl of finely chopped chocolate in a larger bowl (or saucepan) of very hot water. (The water should reach no more than ⅓ of the way up the side of the small bowl.) Be sure the water doesn't touch the chocolate as you gently stir it, then remove the small bowl from its hot-water bath when the chocolate is smooth.

Crystallized Ginger
Ginger was among the first spices adopted by Western cooks and still a favorite. The candied variety so often used in baking is made from small pieces of the root preserved in a sugar syrup and then coated with granulated sugar.

Flour
Most American wheat produces a "hard" flour high in gluten and ideal for bread making. "Soft" flour, though good for cakes, provides less elasticity. For the sake of versatility, *all-purpose flour* is a blend of hard and soft flours and your best choice for general use. *(See Brown Rice Flour.)*

Herbes de Provence
Available at specialty food stores, this mix of dried thyme, basil, savory, fennel and lavender is often used to flavor Mediterranean dishes. Because there are no established proportions for its ingredients, you can just as easily blend a supply to suit your own taste. Like other dried herbs, it keeps best in an airtight container away from direct heat and sunlight.

Mushrooms
Always select plump, firm mushrooms, and keep them refrigerated in a paper bag lined with a paper towel. (Never store them in plastic.)

The most versatile of the brown mushrooms for cooking is the *crimini.* Newer to the marketplace is the rather enormous *portabella,* which is actually a crimini that has been allowed to reach full growth before it's harvested. Both have a full, meaty flavor.

The white *button mushroom* is harvested early in its growth, so the stem is still very short, and the cap is small and rounded. They're equally good cooked or sliced raw in a salad.

Most often sold dried, the *porcini* is an Italian variety with a rich, deep flavor. (To reconstitute dried mushrooms, simply soak them in hot water for 20 minutes.)

Nut Flours
When nuts are ground, the result is a nutritious flour that, although high in fats, is free of cholesterol. With a food processor and one simple precaution, you can easily make your own nut flour: To the whole nuts, add at least two tablespoons of sugar or flour from the recipe before processing to a fine consistency. (Without the additional ingredient, the oil in most nuts will quickly turn them into a nut butter.) Nut flours are also available at natural-foods stores and by mail order.

Oils

The best all-around oil for cooking is a mild vegetable oil. Corn, canola and grapeseed oils are especially good.

The best *olive oils* are generally labeled as "cold-pressed" or "extra-virgin" to distinguish an oil with the least acidity and most natural flavor. Because flavorful oils lose most of their character when heated, cook with any good, fresh olive oil labeled as "virgin," and reserve the expensive ones for seasoning salads and cooked meats and vegetables.

Dark sesame oil is a fragrant oil best reserved for Asian, Indian and Middle Eastern dishes. Its strong flavor tends to clash with the ingredients of other cuisines.

Olives

What with the oil it produces, the little olive is truly the cornerstone of Mediterranean cooking. Both the unripened green olives and tree-ripened black olives must be cured before they're fit to eat. Those plump, supermarket olives cured in lye are no substitute for brine-cured olives; the ones packed in oil are your best choice. *Kalamata olives* are imported from Greece. You'll find them in specialty food shops and some supermarkets.

To easily pit an olive, roll over it with a rolling pin to loosen the seed, which can then be plucked out.

Pine Nuts

The seeds from the cone of a Mediterranean pine, pine nuts are most often used in pesto sauce and Middle Eastern sweets and rice dishes. Toasting them beforehand brings out their flavor. Because pine nuts have a short shelf life, buy in small quantities, and keep them refrigerated.

Potato Starch *(or Potato Starch Flour)*

For those allergic to corn, this is the ideal substitute for cornstarch as a thickening agent. (But the *potato flour* sold by natural-foods stores is too heavy for this use.)

Prosciutto

Pronounced *pro-shoo'-toe,* prosciutto is the Italian word for "ham." But it is unlike any other ham. Dry cured and pressed to give it a flat shape, finely textured prosciutto is usually sold in translucent, paper-thin slices by specialty food stores and well-stocked supermarkets. While there is no ideal substitute for prosciutto in most recipes, country ham or Canadian bacon from a deli will do if it's sliced extremely thin.

Rice

There are many more varieties of rice than the familiar *long-grain white rice.* Aromatic *basmati rice,* another long-grain variety, is the best choice for Middle Eastern and Indian dishes. A short-grain rice such as *arborio* and *carnaroli* is the basis of a true Italian risotto.

Processing rice to remove only its husk results in *brown rice.* The bran that is retained gives it color as well as a nutty taste and chewy texture.

The long, slender dark grains that we call *wild rice* are more accurately the seeds of a native American aquatic grass. Nutritious and smoky flavored, it cooks more slowly than true rice.

Yogurt

Of Persian origin, yogurt is a fermented, semiliquid milk product. Flavored yogurts have proliferated in recent years, but tart-tasting plain yogurt is the cook's choice.

Zante Currants

When they're dried, seedless black Corinth grapes become very flavorful, tiny raisins known as Zante currants. (They should not be mistaken for red and black currants, which are true berries.) When cooking with dried currants, always wash and pat them dry beforehand. Dark raisins make an adequate substitute.

Resources

Ingredients and Cook's Tools

EACH of these enterprises has proven itself reliable in supplying ingredients and wares with courtesy and efficiency. Several operate well-stocked stores in addition to their mail-order business, and you may have better luck in finding exactly what you want through one of their stores. Call the toll-free number for the location of your nearest store.

The Baker's Catalogue
800-827-6836

The makers of King Arthur Flour, a Connecticut brand as old as the nation, publish this amazing catalog. You can rely on them for virtually any baking ingredient or ware, as well as their own exceptional wheat flours.
Brown rice flour, xanthan gum powder, potato starch, Zante currants, nut flours, almond paste, crystallized ginger, chocolate, olive oil sprayer, baking sheets and pans, and baking dishes.

Dean & DeLucca
800-221-7714

What began 20 years ago as a grocery store in New York's SoHo district is today a "neighborhood food emporium" with a wonderful array of fine food and kitchenware, plus a mail-order catalog.
Cheese, oils, dried mushrooms, olives, arborio rice, Herbes de Provence, balsamic vinegar, French lentils, crystallized ginger, chestnut puree, baking chocolate and bakeware.

Lundberg Family Farms
(530) 882-4551

The Lundbergs have grown fine, organic rice in California's Sacramento Valley for well over fifty years. Their basmati, arborio and brown rices are excellent. You can purchase their products in natural-foods stores or by mail order (in 25-pound bags or by the case).

Sur La Table
800-243-0852

A good source for truly professional cookware of every sort and size, Sur La Table has a handful of stores on the West Coast and a mail-order catalog that reaches points east. The selection of bakeware is impeccable.
Natural scallop shells, foil candy and baking cups, baking sheets and pans, pastry bags and tips, meat thermometers, zesters, olive oil sprayers, baking dishes and roasting racks.

Williams-Sonoma
800-541-2233

With stores nationwide and its venerable mail-order catalog, Williams-Sonoma has made its reputation by supplying America's cooks with fine kitchen wares and a choice selection of specialty foods.
Olive oil sprayers, zesters, bulb basters, meat thermometers, roasting racks, pastry bags and tips, crystallized ginger, olive oils, Herbes de Provence, imported chocolate and (on a seasonal basis) fine meats, cheeses and sausages.